GHOSTS OF WINTER

AMY GORDER

Ghosts of Winter

BY

Amy Gorder

Bend, Oregon 2024

Emerald Books
Paperback ISBN: 978-1-954779-97-6

Illustrated by Isaac Peterson

Emerald Books, Bend, Oregon

Emerald Books

For Chris, always

*The real ghost stories are the
histories of the past that take shape
in the present and forever
impact the future.*

Prologue

Houdi awoke to the sound of violin music. He sat up and glanced around the room, paused at the window, and saw a dark shadow looming outside, like a figure looking in. The music seemed to be coming from the shadow. Houdi rubbed his eyes and looked again. Nothing was there. The music stopped. Rain streaked down the glass. Houdi laid his head back on the pillow.

Wind began blowing throughout the room. Trick cards from Houdi's magic kit flew in a circle above him. The dark figure appeared beside Houdi's bed. Its long white hair spilled from a black shroud. It melded with the howling gust and flew about the room. It again stopped beside Houdi's bed. The wind ceased to blow. The ghost swung its head from side to side like a pendulum. A loud tick-tock kept time.

Houdi attempted to shout, but his voice was gone. He buried his eyes in his pillow. His breathing quickened. He told himself it wasn't real. When he gathered enough courage to peek out, the ghost was gone.

A loud screech at the window startled Houdi. He froze. It sent shivers up his spine. He sat up. From outside, the ghost scrawled letters across the window. He mouthed each letter: *M . . . R . . . O . . . T . . . S . . . E . . . H . . . T . . . M . . . A . . . I.* The clock ticked faster, keeping time to Houdi's rising heartbeat.

Houdi jumped from his bed and ran for the door. It slammed shut. He pulled at the doorknob. The ghost reappeared. It lifted a violin and bow and began to play. The haunting melody filled the room. It was full of melancholy and longing. "Heed my words," the ghost wailed above the music.

Words? Were they words? He turned back and willed himself to focus. Then it clicked; they were anadromes, words spelled backward. Houdi reversed the letters and said aloud, "I am the storm."

The ghost stopped playing. "Yesss," it hissed. "I am the storm, Houdi." Houdi ran back to his bed and pulled the comforter over his head.

The shadow followed and grabbed his shoulders, shaking him. "Leave me alone!" he cried.

"Houdi, wake up!" The voice was familiar. He opened his eyes. His mother sat next to him on the bed. He reached up and hugged her.

"That must have been some dream," she said, patting his back.

"It was a nightmare," Houdi replied, wiping sleep from his eyes. He glanced around his room; nothing seemed out of place, and no one was at the window.

"Well, try to shake it off," his mom said. "It's time to get ready for school. Today is the field trip to the Elk Grove Museum, and Mr. Kelly won't like it if you're late."

Houdi's older sister, Amelia, peeked into the room. "Good morning, Houdini."

"Houdi!" he corrected.

"Have fun today. Just don't make anyone disappear, okay?" Amelia grinned. Houdi rolled his eyes. He loved being known for his magic tricks, but not now.

Amelia left the room and said, "See ya later, gators!"

"Goodbye!" their mom replied. She turned back to Houdi. "Are you okay?" He nodded. "Good," she said, ruffling his hair. "I'm off to work. Have fun on the field trip, and don't be late."

Houdi heard the door close downstairs. The house felt eerie and quiet. He dressed and sat on the floor to tie his shoes.

He looked in the mirror. He put on his clear-framed glasses and combed his sandy brown hair. Something in the reflection caught his attention. Houdi turned back to the window behind him. A shiny black crow was perching on the windowsill. It stared at him with its dark, beady eyes. Houdi hurried to the window and tapped on the glass. The crow cawed and flew away.

Houdi looked up at the gray clouds rolling in the morning haze; a storm was coming. As usual, he slipped into his jacket, flung his backpack over one shoulder, and stashed a few magic tricks in his pocket. He hurried down the stairs and out the door. He locked it behind him.

As he walked, the ticking sound returned and kept time to his footsteps. He paused. It stopped. "You're imagining things," he said aloud. But deep down he knew it may be more.

I.

ON DISPLAY

At school, Houdi and Abby waited in line to board the yellow school bus. It was sprinkling rain. The classroom door opened, and their teacher, Mr. Ryan Kelly, hurried out, carrying his coat over one arm and a clipboard in his hand. He strode past the students to the bus door and signaled the driver with a knock. "We're ready to go, Joe!" Joe opened the bi-fold door.

Ryan Kelly climbed the first step and turned back. "Two people to a seat, and I trust that you all know the bus rules by now."

Abby stood behind Houdi in line. "I'm so excited, aren't you?" She hopped a little, unable to contain her joy, which bubbled over. "I can't wait to see inside the new museum. Maybe we'll see a ghost, or the organ will play on its own like people say!"

Houdi shrugged.

"You're excited, too, right?" Abby asked.

"I guess so," he replied.

Abby and Houdi stepped up and walked down the narrow aisle to the back half of the bus and claimed a seat.

"Hey, Houdi, got any magic tricks?" Jace asked from the seat behind. His brown eyes and curly black hair were barely visible above the seat's high back.

"Yeah, show us a trick!" Jace's seatmate, Carlos, added.

Houdi slipped his hand into the pocket of his jeans. He turned around on his knees and held his hands up. "My hands are empty, see?" The boys nodded. Houdi reached past Jace's ear to his curly black hair and pulled his hand out. He held a quarter up for them to see.

"How'd you do that?" Carlos asked.

"It's just between me and Houdini," he said, turning around in his seat. Houdi and Abby could hear the boys discussing it.

"How does he know so many magic tricks?" Carlos asked.

"I don't know," Jace replied. "Sometimes he knows things before they happen, too. Abby calls it his spidey sense."

"So, he's a magician *and* he has ESP?" Carlos asked.

"I think so. Remember when Houdi told us that he dreamed we were all in the classroom, and there was a total sun eclipse, and the sky went dark?" Carlos nodded. "And then, the next day, the power went out at school, and we didn't have lights for the rest of the week, and they canceled school."

"Maybe he *is* Houdini," Carlos said. Abby and Houdi put their hands over their mouths to stifle their laughter.

"Carlos, Houdini died years ago!"

"Maybe he's the *ghost* of Houdini?"

"Dude, he's *real*! A ghost wouldn't be in seventh grade!"

"Well, maybe he's Houdini's grandson," Carlos replied. Jace shrugged and gave up the argument.

The school bus turned and jostled the students in their seats. The last brown leaves of autumn still clung to the branches of the oak trees that met over the road, forming a brown tunnel of twisted limbs.

As the bus drew closer to the museum, Houdi heard a voice inside his head. *Houdi . . .* He shivered.

"Are you okay?" Abby asked.

"Yeah," Houdi replied. "I was thinking about a nightmare I had last night."

"Nightmares are the worst! What did you dream?"

"I dreamed a ghost was outside my window, watching me. Then it was in my room, playing the violin and talking to me. It was so creepy."

"I'm sorry that happened, Houdi!"

The bus turned into the parking lot, and the students' voices grew louder. "Look!" Abby pointed, pressing her cheek against the window. The Elk Grove House and Stage Stop Museum came into view. The brick exterior was a shining example of a beautiful gold rush–era building. The bus rolled up to the walkway and stopped. Joe opened the door.

Ryan stood to face the eager students. "Once you exit the bus, explore the front grounds for a few minutes. This region is home to various plant species, some native to California, while others were brought here by settlers who traveled from all over the world. And don't forget to read the plant labels. They're full of information." He started to exit, then turned back. "One more thing. If you have seen the building before the renovation, look at the changes made to the outside of the building."

Ryan stepped off the bus. The students followed. Houdi paused before taking the final step down. He drew his eyes to the high windows of the building.

"Houdi, *go*!" Jace yelled.

"Give it a rest, Jace," Abby shot back. Jace rolled his eyes.

Abby and Houdi got off the bus. Together with the class, they cut across the vast green lawn. Abby took a deep breath. "It smells so good!"

"It's called petrichor," Houdi said, "the earthy smell after a rain."

"Well," Abby replied, grinning, "whatever it's called, it smells good!"

The flower garden was ablaze with bright red camellia blossoms sparkling in the morning dew. The sweet aroma of narcissus and gardenia flowers filled the air. One plant label grabbed everyone's attention by describing how Native Americans used honey-scented pink manzanita flowers to make cider and jelly. The students pointed out tree squirrels scurrying up and down tall evergreens and robins chirping as they flew overhead.

The building's exterior was restored and revitalized. Old crumbling bricks were replaced with new red ones, and the front porch, balcony, and shutters were new and painted white. Rocking chairs moved with the breeze on the new front porch. And a welcome banner featuring a majestic elk design fluttered in the gentle wind. All these things added a charming touch to the entrance.

"Everyone, please join me at the steps," Ryan called from the porch. He was tossing and catching a green tennis ball. The students knew what that meant and ran to join him. It was the See What You Know game.

He pushed his wind-blown hair back and gestured back at the building. "Cool place, huh?" The students agreed. "Let's review for a moment. Who can explain how the California Gold Rush started and became a global phenomenon?" Hands flew up.

"Give it a go, Jace," Ryan said, throwing the ball to him.

Jace reached up and caught it. "Well, James Marshall discovered gold in the American River and decided to show it to his boss, John Sutter. They wanted to keep it a secret, but it didn't turn out that way."

"Great job!" Ryan replied. Jace returned the ball. "Why didn't it stay a secret?" He tossed the ball to Abby. She caught it with one hand.

"Because the news leaked out, and newspapers published it around the world." She tossed the ball back.

"Right, and who was the first person to publish it?" He threw the ball to Carlos.

"Sam Brannon," Carlos said, throwing it back.

"Okay, what was the name of Sam Brannon's newspaper, and where was it located?"

No hands went up. Houdi looked around and, with some reluctance, raised his hand. Ryan tossed him the ball.

"The *California Star* in San Francisco."

"Do you remember the year, Houdi?" Ryan asked.

"Eighteen forty-eight," he replied and returned the ball.

"That's right, and the news spread like wildfire! The following year, people flooded in worldwide, hoping to strike it rich. Who remembers what people called them?" He cupped his ear and waited for a collective response from the class.

"Forty-niners!"

"Yes! Of course, many forty-niners came for gold, but others came to make their fortune by providing goods and services to the prospectors. And that leads us to Elk Grove. Who remembers the name of the family that built the hotel in 1851?" He cupped his ear again.

"The Hall family!"

Ryan nodded. "James and Sarah Hall constructed this building to serve as both their home and a hotel and stage stop for travelers and their horses to rest and refuel." Ryan was pleased, and it showed. "Well done!"

He opened the entrance door and called to the docent on duty. "Are you ready for us, Mrs. West?" An energetic woman dressed in pioneer clothing joined them on the porch. Her smile was radiant, her voice joyful.

"Hello and welcome! I'm Mrs. West, one of the docents here at the museum. Before you begin your tour, we must review some safety guidelines." She listed them. "Mr. Kelly and I will be your tour guides today. You are fortunate because your teacher is the president of the Elk Grove Historical Society and knows everything about the hotel!"

"Thank you, Mrs. West," Ryan replied. He opened the door. The students entered the foyer.

"Ryan, can I have a quick word with you?" Mrs. West whispered.

"Sure. Is everything okay?"

"There have been some odd things happening inside the hotel that I think you should be aware of." Ryan instructed the students to wait patiently. He and Mrs. West moved out of earshot.

"What's going on?" he asked.

Mrs. West looked concerned. "Strange things . . . When I left yesterday, everything was in place. When I came in this morning, some of the chairs in the dining room were on top of the tables. Someone took books from the dome-top chest and threw them all over the floor. Sparkling lights were here and there. And, worst of all, I thought I heard violin music. I'm frightened, Ryan. I don't think I'm crazy, but maybe I am."

Ryan knew she wasn't crazy. "I'll call you as soon as I can," he said, "but please feel free to lock up when we leave and go." She assured him she would.

Ryan thought of his past encounters with Bob and Jenny. To his knowledge, there had been no sign of them since Amelia and her friends found the gold. What Mrs. West described was different. Bob and Jenny were always helpful and never mischievous. The only thing that sounded familiar was the lights that appeared when Bob and Jenny were near.

Mrs. West and Ryan joined the students in the entryway, and Ryan directed their attention to the wall where pictures of the Hall family were on display. "Back then," he said, "daguerreotype photography was popular. The only problem was it required people to stay still for up to fifteen minutes. That is why none of the Halls were smiling. It was just too difficult to hold a smile for that long." He pointed to each photo.

"Here we see James, his wife, Sarah, daughter Anne Adele, and sons, John, Thomas, and William. The Halls were the proprietors of the Elk Grove Hotel from 1851 to 1859. Some people believe that Mr. Hall chose to name the town Elk Grove after discovering elk horns in a grove nearby. Are there any questions?" Ryan scanned the crowd; no one raised their hand. "Then please follow me to the lobby."

They passed the staircase that led to the second floor. Houdi grew more nervous. He kept a watchful eye out.

Ryan and Mrs. West walked behind the lobby's standing desk. The students gathered in close. Ryan gestured to an old worn book open on the desk. "Here is a ledger dating back to 1851, where guests checked in. Those who could write would sign their names, while those who couldn't would make their mark. Usually an *X*. They settled their bill with cash, gold, or pinches of gold dust. They kept gold dust in sacks called poke bags." Mrs. West held up a poke bag that once belonged to the Halls.

Ryan flipped through the ledger. He located a marked page and pointed to a specific entry. "This signature belonged to a forty-niner named Bob Thornton, also known as Big Bob Thornton because of his impressive height. When we're upstairs, Mrs. West will provide further information about Bob and his fiancée Jenny."

He closed the ledger. His voice grew mysterious. "Some signatures are missing from this ledger. They're missing because they *NEVER* checked in. They also *NEVER* checked out."

Exchanging side glances, the students followed their teacher and the docent down the hall to the dining room.

"Two years ago, four of my students found this trunk." Ryan pointed to a brown dome-top steamer trunk full of old books.

"My sister was one of them," Houdi said.

"That's right," Ryan replied. "Amelia found a small poetry book wedged inside a larger book, buried at the bottom of *this trunk*. She and three classmates discovered clues inside the poetry book that led them to something *BIG*!"

"Gold!" Abby cried.

"Yes, they found nuggets of all sizes and turned them over to the historical society. And because they were so generous, we now have this beautiful museum."

Ryan Kelly had a long history with the hotel. When he was a kid, he and his best friend, Matt Fox, snuck into the abandoned hotel. They came face-to-face with two gentle ghosts, Bob and Jenny, who asked them to help save the hotel from destruction. Despite Matt's fear of ghosts, Ryan was fascinated and vowed to always protect the hotel. Their differing opinions destroyed their friendship for many years.

As adults, Matt, now the mayor of Elk Grove, once ran a campaign to replace the hotel with a golf course. Ryan, now the president of the Elk Grove Historical Society, opposed the campaign. However, when Bob and Jenny intervened and prevented a potential disaster at the hotel, Matt realized the importance of the building's history. Matt and Ryan reconciled, and Matt became a strong advocate of the hotel and a dedicated supporter of the Elk Grove Historical Society.

Ryan rubbed his palms together. "Are you ready to go upstairs? Mrs. West, they're all yours!" The students peeked into each room along the way, while Mrs. West told stories about some of the people who once stayed there.

When they reached the foot of the stairs, Mrs. West said, "These stairs are steep and dangerous, so be careful; we'll gather in room 202." The students followed her up. Abby and Houdi were last in line.

Houdi tapped Abby on the shoulder; she stopped and turned back. "I feel like someone is watching us," he said.

"Who do you think is watching us?" she asked.

Houdi shook his head. "I don't know."

"It could be the nightmare is getting to you," she replied, continuing up.

Houdi was reluctant but followed. He paused when he saw lights hovering above a stair. He continued, watching the lights over his shoulder. He followed the class down the hall. They filed into room 202. Houdi waited outside the door. Mrs. West began to speak. Houdi tiptoed down the hall to the stairs. The lights shone brighter. He walked toward it and drew his eyes in for a closer look.

The glints of light disappeared beneath a gap in the stair tread. Houdi wedged his fingers in the gap and pulled it up with little effort. Something below reflected the lights. He reached inside and tapped something solid. He grabbed it. He pulled his hand out and dropped the object in his pocket. Returning the stair tread to its place, he tamped it down with his foot. He sat on the stairs and pulled out the object. He opened his hand. A gold-plated pocket watch! He saw the initials *J.A.S.* etched into it.

Abby returned to the landing. "Houdi, what are you doing? Come on!" He put the watch in his pocket and hurried to join the class.

Mrs. West was in the middle of her lively presentation, and the students were all ears. "Bob stumbled upon a hidden treasure in the Cosumnes River earlier that day," she said, "and with the fear of bandits lurking around, he decided to spend the night here. Despite taking precautions, he couldn't shake the feeling of being followed. So, to safeguard the gold, he hid it in different parts of this room and jotted down the clues in a poetry book gifted to him by his fiancée, Jenny."

Mrs. West took out a small brown book from a glass display case. "Here is the poetry book Jenny gave Bob when he left Boston and boarded a clipper ship bound for California and the gold fields. Bob needed money to receive Jenny's parents' blessing for their marriage, and he wanted to ensure that Jenny could find the gold if something happened to him. As it turned out, his instincts were spot on."

Mrs. West replaced the book in the display case and picked up a glass perfume bottle with an atomizer. "This was Jenny's rose perfume bottle. We have no proof, but we like to think it was a gift from Bob." She returned it to the display case and continued.

"There weren't any cellphones or social media back then, but they had word of mouth. Everyone talked and relayed information to each other. That's what happened here.

"Rumors of Bob's discovery spread throughout the area. The Skinner brothers, infamous outlaws known for thievery and murder, managed to get hold of information about Bob's whereabouts. They discovered that Bob was en route to Elk Grove on the Lower Sacramento Road and thought he might be staying at the only hotel in the vicinity, the Elk Grove Hotel.

"They rode here and waited in the shadows until they were sure everyone was asleep. George later told Mr. Hall that they knew which room was Bob's because they saw a man who fit his description standing in the window. The brothers waited awhile after the lights went out, then made their move. They shimmied up the oak tree out front to the balcony and climbed in through the open window of Bob's room.

"The Skinners thought this would be easy pickings, but they were wrong. Bob hid the gold so well they couldn't find *one* nugget! The Skinners were furious, and a fight broke out. While attempting to defend himself with his Bowie knife, Bob killed Cyrus, and in retaliation, George shot and killed Bob. The Halls took George as a prisoner and summoned Sheriff Joseph McKinney to the hotel to bring justice to George for killing Bob. The sheriff sentenced George to die for his crimes, and he and Mr. Hall hung him from an oak tree, where his body remained for several days as a warning to others."

The students were quiet. Abby raised her hand. Mrs. West called on her. "Did Jenny ever know about the gold, or the clues Bob left?"

"I'm afraid not. Jenny traveled here hoping to find Bob but learned from the Halls that the Skinner brothers had killed him. She never saw the poetry book again, and she died here, too, from a disease they called consumption back then. Today, it's known as tuberculosis.

"I'm sorry we don't have any photos of Bob or Jenny, but we have more of their belongings. Here is Bob's red flannel shirt," she said, holding her hand out toward the shirt laying on the antique bed. "And on the floor, you see the boots he wore. Jenny's beautiful blue dress is hanging on this dress form, and her carpet bag and black button-up shoes are on the floor beside it." Mrs. West walked briskly across the room.

"Mrs. Hall brought her organ along with her on the Overland Trail. Sometimes, people ask if it plays on its own. But those are just rumors." She stepped up to another display. "This display showcases some of the Halls' other belongings." She pointed out Mr. Hall's spectacles and Mrs. Hall's yellow apron.

She reached behind the case and pulled out a framed picture. "Here is a copy of a daguerreotype of George and Cyrus Skinner." The two young men glaring at the camera captivated the students. They were wearing cowhide chaps and wide-brimmed hats, and clutching revolvers to their chests.

"The Skinner brothers were involved in another unfortunate event, a run-in with a notorious group of bandits led by a man named Joaquin Murietta."

"Mr. Kelly told us about him!" Carlos blurted out. "He was a bandit who stole from people and gave the stuff to poor Mexican people who had no money."

Mrs. West pulled out another copy of a daguerreotype and held it up. A young man with wavy black hair, dark eyes, and a heavy mustache stared back. He wore a serape around his shoulders and, on his head, a sombrero.

"Yes," Mrs. West agreed. "Many Mexicans were abused and forced off their claims. They were not able to make money, so they couldn't return to Mexico. Many *were* starving. Joaquin and his gang of bandidos were outraged by the injustice they saw, and their anger led them down a dangerous path. They became killers and targeted prospectors. They stole whatever they could, including gold, guns, and horses, but instead of keeping all the spoils for themselves, they distributed them to those in need. Joaquin's reputation grew among the Mexican people. Does anyone know what they called him?"

"The Robin Hood of the West!" Jace cried.

"That's right! But not everyone saw Joaquin and his gang as heroes. To many, they were ruthless thieves and would kill for no reason." She turned to Ryan. "Let's cross the hall to the ballroom, and I'll hand it over to you."

The students were amazed by the beauty of the ballroom. The grand hall spanned the entire length of the building. Ornate plaster medallions encircled crystal chandeliers. Gold-flecked wallpaper covered the walls. Red velvet drapes and valances framed the windows that overlooked the grove. Students could see their reflections in the polished floor.

"Imagine dressing up in your finest clothing and dancing all night until sunrise!" Ryan exclaimed. "Back then, attending dances was a popular trend, and everyone wanted to participate.

"As you can see, the historical society did an excellent job recreating the ballroom as it would have appeared years ago. They researched photos and read descriptions written by people who had attended dances here. And by the way, the museum is holding its first-ever Winter Ball in this very ballroom in a couple weeks. There will be music and dancing here again for the first time in over one hundred and fifty years!"

"Are you going to dance until sunrise, Mr. Kelly?" Carlos asked. The class laughed.

"I might," Ryan replied, joining the laughter. "But the purpose of the Winter Ball is to raise money for the second part of the restoration, the stable and the graveyard out back. It's also to honor those who had a part in saving the building from destruction. And for the docents, like Mrs. West, who helped create this beautiful museum and teach about the history."

"There's a graveyard out back?" Houdi asked.

"Yes, there is, but I'm afraid the overgrowth of dirt, grass, and weeds hides the graves. Many people died here or nearby, and this area needed a place to bury the dead."

Outside, lightning flashed, gray clouds rumbled, and rain began to fall. Ryan raised his voice above the downpour. "Everyone, this concludes our tour. It's time to return to the bus." The students groaned and walked out into the hall. Ryan and Mrs. West followed them. They headed down the stairs and out the door to the bus. No one saw Houdi lingering behind, not even Abby. She was talking with a group of girls.

Houdi scanned the ballroom. Violin music began to play. He recognized the same sad tune from his nightmare; it mimicked a howling cat. The ghost materialized. Still shrouded in black, its face and hands were more visible in the light of day: gray skin, hollow eye sockets, and a large gaping mouth.

The ghost stopped playing. It turned slowly toward Houdi. The tick-tock returned. "We meet again, Houdi." His mind raced; it hadn't been a dream at all.

It reached its gnarled gray hand toward him. Long black fingernails extended from each finger and thumb.

It pointed and shrieked, "Do not be a thief of time!" Wind poured from its mouth. The howling force blew Houdi across the room, slamming him against the wall. He slid to the floor.

Glints of light and the scent of roses filled the room. Two ghosts appeared and lifted Houdi to his feet. "Run, Houdi!" they cried. They turned back to the other ghost. They encircled the vile thing, preventing it from moving.

"You cannot outrun me, Houdi; I will *always* find you!"

Houdi raced down the hall, jumped over the stairs, and ran out the open door to the bus.

"Are you okay?" Ryan asked. Houdi did his best to appear unfazed.

"Yeah, I just needed to use the restroom." He hurried down the aisle and found his seat next to Abby.

"Where were you?" Abby asked.

Still breathing hard, Houdi reached into his pocket. He made sure no one was watching, then handed her the watch. "I'm not sure where to begin," he said, his voice thin. He closed his eyes and rested his head on the seatback. The bus surged ahead, taking the class back to school.

Lucy plays a mournful tune

The Wild West

Autumn 1851

2.

OCCURRENCE AT SUTTER'S FORT

"Will you just *go*!" Cy yelled louder than the braying horses. George hollered back, "I'm trying! Do you want me to ride out in front of them?"

"At this point, it's all the same to me!" Cy replied.

George spurred his horse forward. He barely avoided a collision with a massive white ox pulling a bullock cart full of lumber.

"What's the matter with you?" the bullwhacker yelled, struggling to regain control of the panicked ox. "You got a death wish?"

Cy brought his horse to a canter and caught up with George. The horses trotted side by side down the Kay. Cy looked irritated. He shook his head.

"George, I don't know what gets into you."

George never liked disappointing his brother. "Sorry, Cy," he replied, "but you told me to go."

"I told you to go, but I didn't tell you to get killed. Use your head, little brother."

It was cloudy, and rain was falling. Now and then, a glimmer of sunshine broke through. Cy and George wore long dusters over their clothes and cowboy hats they stole from a merchant in the last town they passed through.

Even with the rain, the Kay was bustling with people doing various things. Some walked, some rode horses, and others were in coaches or wagons. George kept his eyes peeled for the fort. He and Cy had never been there before. He was excited to see it for himself.

A man passed by on his wagon. He greeted them. "Howdy do." Cy and George tipped their chins. A young boy sat on the box seat beside the man. His eyes were wide, and he gaped at everything around him.

Two men were in a shouting match. "What do you mean? I don't owe you a blasted thing!" one man shouted. He was burly and towered over his rival in a threatening stance.

"Yeah, nah, yeah, mate!" The other man replied. He had arrived from Australia the week before. The fight was over a gambling debt the burly man had yet to pay. They agreed to fisticuffs.

They unfastened their gun belts and threw them aside. They lifted their fists. They circled each other. Some people gathered to cheer the fight on. One man was busy taking bets.

Cy and George stopped to watch. The burly man threw the first punch. Blood trickled down the Aussie's face. The burly man attempted to strike another blow. The Aussie kneed him in the gut.

"Is that all you've got?" the burly man taunted.

"Shut your cakehole, you wanker!" the Aussie replied and wrestled him to the muddy ground. He straddled him. He threw one blow after another to the burly man's face. The burly man stopped fighting. His eyes were swollen shut; he couldn't see to fight. The man taking bets held up the Aussie's fist and declared him the winner. The crowd cheered.

"If I ain't paid by tomorrow, there'll be more of the same, you yobbo! You can bet on it!" the Aussie said, putting his gun belt back on. He pointed at the man. "Never underestimate an Aussie from the bush."

George and Cy continued up the Kay. A stagecoach was approaching in the opposite direction. Many on the road shouted, "Hi, Charley!" as the stagecoach passed. The driver grinned and waved in return.

George called to a man passing them on his horse. "Hey, who's that guy driving the stagecoach?" The man pulled back the reins, and his horse stopped. George and Cy stopped, too.

"That's Charley Parkhurst," he replied. "Best stage driver in these parts. He knows all about horses. Many people won't take a stagecoach unless Charley's the driver."

They rode on. The white walls appeared in the distance. George sat up straight in his saddle. He shielded his eyes from the sun as the stark white walls came into view.

"Is that it, Cy?" George pointed.

"I suppose it is, little brother. Sutter's Fort right there."

They arrived at the fort and rode up to the stable. They dismounted and handed the reins to the stable hand, a young Miwok boy. Entering through the south gate, they saw Hawaiian Kanakas working to construct a more substantial barrier at the entrance. Maidu and Miwok women washed the soldiers' clothes in the covered area. And their children were outside the fort, making wicks and dipping them in melted fat to make candles.

Many shops were open to offer various goods and services. Prospectors streamed in and out of the trade store. Those exiting had their arms piled high with necessities. Many carried mining and panning equipment. Others waited at the blacksmith's shop for newly forged horseshoes to take to the farrier. A long line snaked around the blacksmith's shop where enthusiastic pioneers and prospectors waited to have their flintlock muskets repaired or to catch a glimpse of the new muzzle-loading long-barreled shotgun. A line formed in front of the bakery for black acorn bread and fry bread made by Native women.

California militia soldiers patrolled inside and outside the fort walls to keep the peace. Their uniform coats were dark blue, the cuffs, collars, and pants light blue. Their dark blue hats were made of felt with black ostrich feather plumes. George and Cyrus paid particular attention to the muskets they carried. Neither brother said a word to the other, but they noted it all the same.

"Maybe we'll catch a glimpse of John Sutter, Cy."

"Maybe, but we're not here to look for *him*."

"Oh, I know, but I reckon seeing him might be kind of exciting."

"Keep your focus, George. We got work to do."

George shrugged.

Passing by the Vaquero Room, they saw the lively vaqueros getting ready to ride out to Sutter's Hock Farm. The riders were busy buckling up their chaps and looping the lariats they would use to rope the cattle.

Cyrus pulled George closer. "I heard the head vaquero, a Miwok man named Olimpio, is also the keeper of the keys while Sutter's away. That could be him near the door. He's talking, and they're listening. We have to keep an eye out for him."

"Okay, Cy," George replied.

George's stomach growled as he breathed in the aroma of the fresh-baked bread wafting through the courtyard. "Do you think we can go to the bakery, Cy? I'm mighty hungry."

Cy turned sharply and spoke in a low, no-nonsense tone. "No, we're not here to eat or to see John Sutter. You've got to focus, or we'll both be in hot water. You hear?"

"Yeah, I suppose," George said, rubbing his stomach.

They stopped outside the carpenter's shop. A man was busy sanding a wooden door beneath a canopy. He stopped to remove his wide-brimmed hat, wipe his face with his neckerchief, and replace it. He nodded in their direction. "Hello," he said.

"What are you makin'?" George asked.

"This door's for Sutter's quarters; he said it needs to be sturdier. Got to keep out the riffraff!" He chuckled and removed his worn leather glove, holding his hand out to shake. Cy and George returned the gesture. "Are you two staying at the fort?" the man asked.

"No, just here for the day, then back to the embarcadero," Cy replied.

"Well, that's good, too! Nice to meet you boys. My name's James Marshall."

"By golly, I know who *you* are!" George exclaimed. "You're that fellow who found gold in the American River! I would think you'd be living the high life, and instead, you're working here."

"Oh, I won't be here much longer; I'm just doing a favor for Sutter. I'm fixin' to head to Kelsey's Diggings up in El Dorado. My partner and I just bought a mine north of Chili Bar."

"I see," Cy said, distracted by a man walking up the outside steps of a two-story adobe building in the center of the yard. Marshall followed Cy's gaze.

"That's John Sutter's office and personal living quarters," Marshall said. "He invited me up there for dinner once after the gold discovery. It's very comfortable; only the best for Sutter," he winked.

"The clerk's office is up there, too. The clerk's name is Heinrich Lienhard. He's Swiss, like Sutter. And if you've got a health issue, Doc Gildea has an office there."

A group of young militia soldiers taking a break from patrolling huddled in the yard, talking and laughing. Marshall shook his head. "I sure hope nothing ever happens where we *do* need those soldiers.

Cy narrowed his eyes. "Has this fort ever been attacked for real?"

"Nah," Marshall scoffed, "there's never been any real trouble other than minor distractions. The soldiers are mostly protecting Sutter when he's here."

"Is he here now?" George asked.

"Yeah, that was him just climbing those steps."

"Well, I think we'll head up those steps, too," Cy replied. "I'm assuming there's goods for sale in the clerk's office."

"Oh sure," Marshall said. "Pots, barrels, blankets, ropes, and other things."

"Much obliged," Cy said, already walking toward the building.

"Alright, boys, take it easy," Marshall called after them. "It's raining, so keep your powder dry." Then, as an afterthought, he yelled, "Hey, if you're lookin' for work, you can join us up at the mine. We could use some extra hands."

George turned back to Marshall, lifted his hat, and hurried to catch up with Cy. They climbed the steep steps of the central adobe.

A bell jingled on the door as they entered. Handwritten signs hung above each office door, but the words had no meaning; they never attended school and never learned to read or write.

Cyrus and George had always lived on the lam. Their mother knew how to read and write but wasn't interested in teaching them. She was more concerned with making a living by stealing from others. With no father in the picture, it was just Lucy and her boys. They moved quickly from town to town, taking what they could. The boys had just been along for the ride until they learned the family business, and at a young age, they learned it well.

The brothers entered the foyer and opened the door closest to the entrance, which happened to be the clerk's office. The clerk was busy waiting on a customer seeking answers about hand lamps for the gold mines.

"I'll be right with you, boys," the clerk said.

George moved shoulder to shoulder with Cy. "Are you going to help yourself to any of this?" he whispered.

"Hm, maybe this twine and some of these hooks," Cy said, skillfully slipping them into his pocket.

George's face brightened. "We could do the same at the bakery, Cy. They won't miss a small piece of fry bread."

"I already told you no," Cy whispered back.

The clerk walked up behind them. "Is there anything I can help you boys find?"

"We were lookin' for some twine and hooks," Cyrus replied, "but these here are not the right kind."

"I'm afraid those are the only ones I carry. Did you look at the trade store?"

"Not yet," Cy replied.

A well-dressed middle-aged gentleman with graying hair and a walrus mustache threw the clerk's door open. He barreled into the room, waving a paper. Cy and George recognized him from the steps outside. It was John Sutter. His temper was flaring.

"What is this, Heinrich?" Sutter shouted. "They're charging too much for these pickaxes! Shovels, too!"

Heinrich shook his head. "John," he pleaded, "it's the price they're going for."

"Well, we'll see about that!" Sutter cried. "To be useful to me, Heinrich, you *must* strike a bargain." The clerk sighed, and the scolding continued.

Cy tapped George's arm and whispered, "Come on!" They walked out to the foyer. Cy closed the clerk's door. Only one other door was left open.

Cy turned to face George and gripped his shoulders. "Brother, I'm going to ask you to do something, but you can't draw attention to yourself, you hear me?"

"Yeah."

"Go get both of our horses from the stable and ride west down the Kay toward the embarcadero. When you're almost there, wait under an oak tree on the north side of the road for a reasonable amount of time. If I don't show up, take the horses to the embarcadero and hide where no one can find you. Got it?"

"Okay," George answered, "but you better show up, Cy." Cy reached up and held the bell to keep it from ringing. George opened the door, slipped out, and descended the steps. Cy left the door open in case he required a quick getaway. He could still hear Sutter and Heinrich's muffled voices inside the clerk's office.

Cyrus knew the time was right. He raced into Sutter's office and searched for something, *anything* of value he could take without drawing attention. His eyes swept across the bookshelf, then moved to the desk covered in papers. He pushed the papers to the floor, and there, in the center of the desk, was the *something* he was hoping for, a *gold pocket watch on a gold chain.* Cy couldn't believe his luck. He stashed the watch in his pocket and walked out casually to avoid arousing suspicion should he encounter someone in the foyer. To his relief, Sutter remained in the clerk's office.

George waited under an oak tree on the Kay, biting his thumbnail. His eyes darted back and forth, watching for any sign of Cy. "Please come back, Cy," he said over and over under his breath. Behind him, the sound of footsteps on dry leaves startled him. He pulled his gun and turned around, aiming.

"It's me, George!" Cyrus said, dashing out from the trees. He untethered the reins of his horse and put his foot up into the stirrup. He threw his leg over the horse and settled into the saddle. They clicked their tongues, and their horses trotted on. They both agreed it was safer to take J Street than the Kay back to the embarcadero.

3.

Holding Down the Fort

"My watch! My pocket watch is gone!" John Sutter shouted. The timid clerk ran across the hall to Sutter's office.

"Who could have done this, Heinrich?"

"Whoever it was must have taken it while you were across the hall yelling—I mean, talking to me."

Sutter ignored Heinrich and raised his voice again. "Who has been up here this morning?"

"Well, only a few customers," Heinrich shrugged. "A guy bought some oil lamps."

Doc Gildea rushed in. "What's going on, John?" he asked, peering over his spectacles.

Sutter gestured toward the floor. "Someone came into my office and threw all these papers on the floor, then stole my pocket watch! It was a gift from my father years ago, a parting gift when I left Switzerland!"

"I don't know, John," Doc said, shaking his head. "I've not had any patients yet today." He turned to Heinrich. "Have you seen anyone up here?"

"Only one paying customer," the clerk replied, then remembered, "Oh, and two young men came in and looked around. They didn't stay long and didn't buy—"

Sutter interrupted, "Were they in your office when I was there?"

"Yes, they left while you were there, too."

"Sutter stroked his beard. "It has to be them." He looked at Heinrich. "Would you be able to identify them?"

The clerk nodded. "I probably could."

"What do you mean *probably*?" Sutter exclaimed, throwing his arms up in frustration. "This is a serious matter! It could be the five Joaquins!"

Heinrich shook his head. "No, John, it wasn't Joaquin Murietta's gang. They're Mexican. The boys I saw were white."

Sutter looked back and forth between the two men as he considered his next move. "Alert the soldiers and have them shut down the fort *immediately*! The thieves could still be inside. I'll personally offer a five-dollar gold coin to anyone with information that leads to the capture of the thieves and an additional five dollars if they find the watch." Doc and Heinrich rushed out and gathered the soldiers together. In minutes, the soldiers had secured the south gate and searched the entire fort, with no sign of the thieves.

Outside in the courtyard, James Marshall stopped to talk to the soldiers. "They looked similar and could have been brothers, but they never told me their names. They were both tall, with brown hair under cowboy hats. They carried guns, but that's not unusual. They were particularly interested when I told them that John Sutter was the man walking up the steps of the central adobe. They couldn't get over there fast enough."

"Did they enter the central adobe?" a soldier asked.

"They seemed interested in going to the clerk's office."

As Marshall recounted the details of the two men, Olimpio, the trusted keeper of the keys, stood by listening to every word. When Marshall finished, Olimpio raced up the steps of the central adobe to inform Sutter, who was sitting at his desk putting his paperwork back in order. Olimpio didn't wait for Sutter to invite him in.

"Boss, I think I might know who those boys are."

Sutter looked up. "I'm listening."

"Last night, a group of us were at the River City Saloon. A wanted poster was hanging on the door."

"What poster?"

"The poster showed two men wanted for murder and theft throughout California, the Skinner brothers. It could be those two. The description on the poster seems to match Marshall's description."

"Is a bounty offered?"

"Five hundred for both or two fifty each for delivery to the jail in Sacramento."

Sutter sat back in his chair. "Who's offering the bounty?"

"Governor Burnett. The Skinners are wanted in Texas, too."

"All right, good work, Olimpio. This is why *you* are the keeper of the keys. I can always count on you to keep an eye out and your ear to the ground."

"Yes, sir, Boss, thank you."

"Saddle up and go to the embarcadero. See what you can find out and watch for these scoundrels. Also, see if there are any more posters of them around. We can hang posters here, too." He added, "And one more thing. Stop in at the *Sacramento Union* newspaper. Have them run an ad offering the reward I mentioned. Five dollars for information and another five if they find the watch. Be sure to say it was stolen here at the fort."

Olimpio rushed to the stable and saddled his horse. Without wasting time, he galloped down the busy Kay to the embarcadero, where the streets were abuzz with activity. The land breeze caused him to hold onto his hat.

After securing his horse to the hitching ring, he entered the River City Saloon. It was filled with loud and rowdy men, even though it was morning. Olimpio scanned the door and the walls but couldn't find the wanted poster that had hung on the door the night before. He sat at the end of the bar and watched the bartender wipe down the back bar. The bartender turned to Olimpio and threw the bar towel over his shoulder.

"It's a little early in the day for you, Olimpio. What'll you have?"

"Sure is, Pete. I'll take a lager." He paused. "And some information." Olimpio reached into his vest pocket and placed a coin on the bar. Pete glanced down at the coin and then back at Olimpio. Without picking it up or saying a word, he turned to fill a glass with lager.

"I noticed the wanted poster is gone," Olimpio said, pointing toward the door. "Did you tear it down? Or were the Skinners here and tore it down themselves?"

"Can't say for sure." Pete shrugged.

Olimpio took out another coin and laid it beside the other. "They're young, scraggly looking."

Pete scoffed. "Olimpio, that describes most men who come in here."

Olimpio leaned over the bar and moved close to Pete's ear. "Look, Sutter sent me; you must tell me what you know. Otherwise, Sutter will see that you don't have a job in the morning."

Olimpio sat back on the barstool and tapped his finger on the bar, punctuating the words. "Have. You. Seen. Them?" He slapped down another coin and took a long drink, watching Pete over the rim of the glass.

Pete gazed over the saloon and then back to Olimpio. He leaned in. "Okay, yeah, I saw them," he replied, his voice barely audible. He picked up the coins, put them in his pocket, and continued. "They tore the poster down, but that's all I'm saying. I don't need more trouble; those guys are stone-cold killers. I'm lucky they didn't kill *me*." He poured more lager into Olimpio's glass and set it on the bar.

"What do you mean, *more* trouble?" Olimpio asked.

"Look, they came in late last night after you left. They saw the poster, came after me, roughed me up, and insisted I buy them several tequila shots. They thought I'd put the poster up, but I didn't, and I'm not saying who did."

Olimpio finished his lager and stood up. He pulled another coin from his pocket and laid it on the bar and tipped his black hat. "See you later, Pete."

"Take care, Olimpio," Pete called after him. Olimpio raised his hand without looking back, burst through the swinging doors, and climbed up on his horse.

Exploring the streets, he deftly avoided the deep puddles from the destructive flood three months prior. The odor of the stagnant river water and the damp wood of the buildings still hung heavy in the air.

Riverboats were docked along the waterfront, some passengers embarking and others disembarking. People lined up to use the overflowing outhouses, and some, unwilling to wait, chose to relieve themselves in the open.

He was captivated by the stagecoach drivers, who navigated their horse-drawn coaches through the busy streets, transporting passengers and freight. From the side of the road, people called out to the drivers, waving as they passed by.

Olimpio noticed men hurrying in and out of shops, carrying various supplies and necessities for gold panning or placer mining and securing them to their pack mules or horses. The Huntington-Hopkins Hardware Store, an impressive three-story building, was exciting to him. It sold every manner of hardware and woodenware imaginable.

The Boudin Sourdough wagon attracted a crowd eager to purchase a fresh loaf of bread. Out in front of Luzena Wilson's boarding house was a sign that declared the best food in town, including homemade biscuits, gravy, and cornbread. The Old Tavern, the first brewery in the city, was packed. Olimpio made a mental note to return to those places.

The Chinese laundry was bustling with activity. Steam billowed from its doors. Next door, the Chinese herbal shop displayed a large red sign announcing its opening. The barbershop across the road advertised various services: haircuts, tooth extractions, bloodletting, and even minor surgeries.

And it was evident to Olimpio that there were many more men than women in all the places he passed. To him, Sutter's Embarcadero was alive with golden hopes and dreams, some realized and some shattered.

During the day, Olimpio searched every saloon at the embarcadero but one, the Stinking Tent Saloon. He rode up, dismounted, and tethered his horse. He heard shouting from inside. A small man flew out the canvas flap door, landing on his back just short of Olimpio's horse. Another man, more muscular and powerful, followed and straddled the man's body, punching his face with his enormous fist. Several men spilled out the canvas door to watch.

The man on the ground held his skinny arms over his face to block the blows, but that didn't help. Blood streamed from his face and mouth. "Okay! Okay!" he hollered after each blow. "You're knocking my teeth out!"

The bartender came outside. "Frank, get off him! What are you doing?" The robust bartender pushed Frank off and helped the man up.

"You're a cheat, Ed!" Frank yelled. "And if I come across you again, you'll be in worse shape!"

"Go on home, Ed," the bartender demanded.

"I ain't got no home!" Ed yelled back.

"Then get to your tent and sleep it off, and don't come back here!" the bartender replied.

The man spat blood and limped off down the road. Onlookers followed the bartender and Frank back into the saloon. Olimpio waited for a spell to let everyone settle inside, then entered the hazy, smoke-filled tent. Oil lamps were positioned on the tables and the back bar. Men filled every poker table, throwing back drinks. Two saloon girls dashed back and forth from the bar to the tables.

Olimpio sized up the room. There were no posters of the Skinners. He sat at the bar and ordered a drink, then gazed at the men, looking for two who might fit the description. No one did. He took one last swig of his drink and walked out.

The afternoon air was chilly, and Olimpio felt a sprinkle of rainfall on his cheeks. He pulled his duster from his saddlebag and put it on. He pushed his hat down tighter on his head. Untethering his horse, he straightened the reins and mounted up.

Looking ahead, Olimpio spotted an unusual person riding toward him. He signaled his horse to walk on. As the person drew closer, he saw it was a woman. She didn't seem bothered by the rain and sat tall in her saddle. He thought her clothes were odd, more like a man's clothing than a woman's. She carried something over her back. Olimpio tipped his chin when they passed. The woman nodded.

Olimpio turned his horse east toward the Kay. He couldn't help looking back over his shoulder one last time.

4.

THE STINKING TENT SALOON

Lucy Skinner rode into Sutter's Embarcadero astride her horse, Prince. As was the custom, she nodded at those on horseback as they passed. Lucy knew they didn't know what to make of her but didn't care. She was unapologetically herself.

Lucy wore men's apparel. Her leather doublet fit close to her body. Her crimson breeches gathered at the knee, and she had tucked them inside her tall boots. She wore her long gray hair styled in a braid down her back. A feathered cap sat upon her head. She chewed tobacco and spit along the road. A violin case hung over her back. Inside was the only thing her father left her when he died. She always kept it with her.

She wasn't at the embarcadero to shop for supplies or equipment. Prospecting wasn't something her impatience would allow. She was there to meet two men at the Stinking Tent Saloon. And she couldn't wait to give them the newfound information.

With the reins in one hand and Prince's mane in the other, Lucy slid off the horse to the ground. Few men could match her skill with horses. She was also an expert with the Pepperbox revolver she had tucked in a sash around her waist.

Lucy tied the reins to the hitching post and looked up and down the street, scouting for any threat. Avoiding mud puddles, she pushed the canvas flap door aside and entered. She waited for her eyes to adjust to the dark, smoky tent. The smell of mildew, fire water, and men who hadn't bathed for weeks or months didn't faze her.

Men were focused on their card games. Saloon girls served them drinks. A man played an out-of-tune piano, bobbing his head to the rhythm. Whenever he caught a customer's attention, he flashed a toothless grin and raised his chin toward the tip jar beside him.

Heads turned toward Lucy, and everyone stopped what they were doing. The toothless man stopped playing. The girls stopped serving. The bartender waited. Lucy was used to that reaction. She helped herself to an empty seat at the bar. The men turned back to their card games. The toothless man played the twangy piano again. Loud voices called for more firewater.

"What'll you have?" the bartender asked, not making eye contact with Lucy. He was older; his face was grizzled and his mustache and beard were gray. He wore a worsted vest over his pinstriped shirt. Sleeve garters prevented his blousy sleeves from getting in the way. He wiped his hands on his once-white apron.

"Give me a coffin varnish," Lucy replied.

He poured it and set it on the bar. Lucy downed the drink.

Cyrus and George pushed back the flap door and entered the tent. They pulled their neckerchiefs down from their mouths but left their hats on low to their eyes. They had torn down the wanted posters with their pictures the night before, but they still feared they would be recognized.

They spotted their mother at the bar and joined her.

"Hello, boys," she said. They didn't answer. She turned to the bartender. "Three of the same." They waited for the drinks and left their money on the bar.

Cy and George followed Lucy through the crowd to a table in the back, away from other people.

"What do ya want, Ma?" Cyrus asked.

Lucy smirked. "Can't a mother just *want* to see her children?"

"Since when do *you* just wanna see *us*?" George replied.

"Since today. I heard some news you'll both be interested in."

Cyrus laughed. "You still have that motherly way about you, Lucy. There's always an angle."

He waved to a saloon girl who came to their table. Cy held up three fingers. The saloon girl didn't smile or say anything. She walked back to the bar.

"Just spill it, Lucy," Cy said. "You got us a job or what?"

She pulled her chair in closer. Cy and George did the same.

"There's a man here in California. He's originally from Sonora, Mexico. There's a rumor he's been hiding out. His name is Joaquin Murietta. He's the leader of a gang of bandidos. They call themselves the five Joaquins because they share the same first name. They go by their last names, but I can only remember Murietta. A few other bandidos ride along with them."

Lucy took a drink and continued. "All of them are cold-blooded murderers and thieves."

"Oh, I see," Cy chuckled, "kindred spirits."

"Stuff it, Cy," Lucy replied. "They robbed some prospectors a few days ago in Calaveras. They killed the prospectors and got away with their gold. I heard it's an enormous amount."

"Any idea where they're hiding?" Cy asked.

"No idea, but if I were you, I'd look in the foothills around Calaveras. There are a lot of caves there. They make good hiding places. The Mexican people here know Murietta as the Robin Hood of the West. He gives them money, gold, food, horses, whatever they can steal from prospectors. The Mexican people *will* protect him and the bandidos."

The saloon girl returned with the drinks. She set them on the table, and they paid. When she walked away, Lucy turned to George.

"This is a serious job. Are you sure you're ready for it, Georgie boy?"

"Well, yeah," George replied, shrugging.

"All right, then find them. If anyone can track them down, it's you two. Be quick about it. They'll be looking to jump a riverboat and hightail it back to Mexico before they're found and hanged. They're sure to take the gold with them."

Cy pulled his newly acquired pocket watch from his trousers. He checked the time and laid it down on the table. Lucy reached for it. Cy attempted to grab it first, but Lucy was faster. She snatched it up.

"Thank you, boys! I've always wanted a pocket watch, and this one will do just fine."

"It's our watch, Ma!" George exclaimed. "Cy stole it today at the fort right off Sutter's desk."

"George! Keep your voice down," Cy warned.

"Your brother's right, George," Lucy said. "Don't say anything about this to anyone but us. Understand?" George nodded.

"I'm checking into the Union Hotel for the night," she said. She looked down at the pocket watch. Cyrus and George exchanged a look. "When you find out something worth knowing, leave a note at the front desk." She took a last drink. "I *love* this pocket watch! I can't thank you enough!"

"If word gets around that I took that watch, I'll be a dead man," Cyrus snapped.

"And we didn't give it to you," George added. "You helped yourself to it."

"It's too valuable for you boys to keep; you might lose it," Lucy replied. "Look here," she said, turning the watch over, "it says Swiss Movement Made in Switzerland. It's eighteen-karat gold, engraved with John Augustus Sutter's initials, JAS. And now it's *mine!*" She glared at them, her dark eyes flashing.

Cyrus answered through gritted teeth. "You stole it from us."

Lucy laughed. "Poor Cy. His mama doesn't love him." Her face filled with disgust. "You're a big baby."

"Can you get us a room at the Union, too, Ma?" George butted in, attempting to distract her and defuse her growing anger.

"Do you have money or gold to pay for a room?" George's face dropped. He shook his head. Lucy showed no compassion. "Yeah, that's what I thought. And the answer is no."

A young man jumped from his chair. He began yelling at an older man who sat across from him at a poker table. "You worthless scum!" the young man cried, throwing his drink in the older man's face. The piano man stopped playing. Those in the bar, including the brothers and Lucy, stood and pulled their guns out. Hammers cocked. Every voice was silent.

Lucy tucked her new watch in her sash. Every eye turned toward her. She looked at Cy and George as if to say *Get out before you're recognized.*

She strolled across the room and laid her revolver on the piano lid. The workers and patrons watched her pull the violin case from her back and place it beside the gun. She opened the lid and removed the violin and bow from the case. Facing the crowd, she began to play "Oh, California." As she played, she thought, *If anyone recognizes the boys, I will use the Pepperbox. Nothing can happen to them, at least not until they steal the gold, and I have it in my possession.*

The piano man was confused. Lucy looked at him and nodded. His eyes lit up. He grinned and joined her. The men un-cocked their guns and returned them to their holsters. They dealt new cards. Saloon girls carried more drinks to the tables.

Cy and George threw back their drinks, pulled their neckerchiefs over their mouths and noses, and walked toward the door. On the way out, they glanced at Lucy.

"Same old drill," Cy said, jumping on his horse.

"Ain't it the truth," George replied.

The horses strolled through the embarcadero and headed southeast toward the caves of the Calaveras foothills.

Those still in the saloon never suspected they just had a close brush with the notorious Skinner brothers. Or that they were tapping the toes of their boots to the music of an aging but dangerous crook—their mother, Lucy.

The Skinner Brothers

5.

BAD COMPANY

Wispy clouds rolled across the silvery moon in the dark sky. A horned owl hooted from its perch high above. The night air was foggy and damp.

Cyrus and George hid among the rush grass that grew along the bank of the Calaveras River. They watched an open cave on the other side. Boulders of many sizes piled high to the left of the cave. The bandidos' horses stood in the dark on the right side. Now and then, the horses whinnied.

A bright fire was burning inside the cave. The men, who were speaking Spanish, were loudly conversing and laughing. Cy and George were sure they had found the hideout of Joaquin Murietta and his gang of bandidos. They searched the rocky hills, caverns, and multiple caves in Calaveras, but Mexican men inhabited none until now.

Cy and George watched a man stoke the fire with the toe of his boot. He added another log. The others were making themselves comfortable. They sat and laid on hides or blankets. Empty and half-full bottles of fire water were everywhere on the ground.

The cave eventually grew quiet. The men slept. The bright fire turned to glowing embers.

The winter air turned cooler. Heavier fog rolled in, and mist rose from the river.

The bandidos' lookout sat on a boulder in front of the cave. The lookout held a revolver in one hand and a bottle in the other. His head turned from side to side, watching and listening for any sign of trouble. Cy and George had hopes he would fall asleep, too. By and by, the lookout's chin bobbed against his chest. Then, it rested. He began to snore.

"I'm going to cross and go in," Cy whispered. "Stay on this side of the river, George. Get our horses and tie them further upstream by the sandbar. You can get them later. Come back here as fast as you can. I'm counting on you to cover me."

"Are you sure about this, Cy?" George whispered back.

"Yes, we need the gold so we can eat. Besides, if we don't get it, we'll never hear the end of it from Lucy."

"But Cy, we don't know if they even *have* the gold. You're taking a big risk that may not pay off."

"I'll be fine. Just move the horses and get back here quick, okay?"

"All right," George replied.

The brothers moved upstream. George tended to the horses. Cy held his gun and removed his ammo belt. He held them above the water and crossed at the sandbar, a shallow point in the river. He was careful not to make any splashing sounds.

George ran back to the vantage point. He checked his ammo. He watched and waited.

On the other side, Cy crept up to the cave. He slunk past the sleeping lookout and paused by the boulders. He peeked around the opening. The men still slept. The embers glowed.

One man lay on his back closest to the fire. He wore a heavy sarape. A bulging saddlebag laid beside him. Cy recalled the man's picture on the wanted posters. He had no doubt this man was Joaquin Murietta.

Cy gauged the best path through the sleeping men and the quickest getaway. He was aware that his life would end if he got it wrong. Cy pulled back to think it over. He could leave now, but backing out had never been his style.

Cy took a deep breath and rounded the mouth of the cave. He snaked his way through the sleeping bodies. A bandido snored and rolled over. Cy pointed his gun at the man and froze. The man mumbled something in Spanish. Cy glanced at the other men. They were unfazed by the noise. He walked on toward the leader.

Cy reached Murietta. He slowly lifted the heavy saddlebag. Murietta turned over. His body faced the fire. Cy paused. The leader slept. Cy turned toward the mouth of the cave. He neglected to see the half-full bottle on the ground. He knocked it over. The bottle rolled to the fire. The liquid spilled over the embers. Cy ran. The bottle exploded. The flames burned high.

Outside, the lookout awoke. He saw Cy flee with the saddle-bag. He shouted, "*¡Intruso!* Intruder!"

From across the river, George aimed and fired. The lookout fell. George moved to another position on the bank of the river. He knew the bandidos could see muzzle blast, a reddish glow from his revolver when he fired. Moving after each shot in the dark gave the appearance that there were several gunmen.

More men ran out. George fired one, two, three, four, five, moving each time. Five men dropped.

Another man shouted, "*¡El oro! ¡Se ha llevado el oro!* The gold! He's taken the gold! *¡Encuéntrelo y quien lo robó!* Find it and whoever stole it!"

Cy scurried up the boulders. The bandidos spotted him. They fired. A bullet nicked Cy's leg. He felt a painful sting. George fired. The bandidos tumbled to the ground.

Cy crawled up the rest of the way. He could feel blood running down his leg. The sting was now an unbearable ache. He had difficulty dragging the saddlebag behind him.

At the top, Cy turned to face the rocks. He descended feet first on his hands and knees. He felt for a space large enough to hide the saddlebag. He found one. He pushed the saddlebag in as far as it would go.

He crawled over the last boulder and hobbled through the trees. He heard bats in the distance and walked toward the sound. He was relieved to find an empty cave. He entered. The bats stopped squeaking. He could see their eyes watching him in the darkness. Cy eased his body down and leaned back against the cave wall.

Five men remained inside the bandidos' cave. George watched them pack their saddlebags. "The Five Joaquins," he said under his breath. He bent down and reloaded. The volume of their voices intensified. George looked up. The Joaquins were riding away on their horses. They led the dead bandidos' horses along with them. Many of the horses snorted.

To George, the men appeared as moving shadows in the foggy darkness. He fired in their direction. He ran toward the sandbar. A man yelled, "*¡Estoy golpeado!* He shot me!" George could hear the tramping of horses' hooves. He didn't know if they were running away or toward him. He hid in the trees.

It grew eerily quiet. George saw their shadows crossing downstream. With his gun out, he ran back and moved closer. He fired. A man cried out. George heard a splash in the river. He raised and fired once more. He heard another cry.

George hurried back upstream to the sandbar. He listened and watched. An owl hooted. He untethered his and Cy's horses and crossed the river. He tied them out of sight and raced back to the cave.

A sliver of orange rose in the eastern sky. The fog was dissipating. George made it to the boulders and imitated a dove call, something he and Cy did when they were boys. He heard no response. He climbed over the boulders. He made the dove call again. A weak call returned. He spotted a cave ahead. He ran toward it and made the dove call again. A dove call resounded.

George ran inside the cave. Cy lay on the ground. George bent over him. "Cy, it's me. Where are you hurt?"

Cy opened his eyes. "My right leg. I think it's just a nick. The bullet didn't land. It's bled a lot. I'll need a little help from you."

"Okay, Cy, whatever you need." George tore a strip of lining from his duster and tied it a few inches above Cy's bullet wound.

"I got the saddlebag," Cy said. "The bandidos shot me when I was climbing the boulders beside the cave. I pushed it into a crevice between two large boulders. The boulders and the space are on this side of the rock pile. I moved the saddlebag out of sight, so you'll have to feel for it. It's in there tight. Leave me here and find it before they find us. I'll be okay. Don't you worry."

George wasted no time. He ran from the cave and crawled up the boulders on his hands and knees. Spotting a crevice, he scrambled over and reached his hand inside. He felt a space. George thrust his hand in further.

His fingers touched something. He took hold and felt it move in his hand. He quickly pulled his hand out. He didn't have to see it to know it was a snake. And if it was a rattler, he felt lucky. He knew they were sleepy during the cooler weather and moved very slowly.

George felt for a space on the other side. He prayed it wasn't another snake den. Something was there. He rubbed it between his thumb and forefinger. It felt like leather. The bag was full and stuck. George wiggled it back and forth and yanked it until it broke free. He ran back.

"I got it, Cy."

"Good, brother, now let's get out of here. Those bats are creepy. They're watching me. They must think I'm dinner."

"I hear something, Cy," George whispered. He put his finger to his lips. "Wait here." He laid the saddlebag down and pulled out his gun. He peeked around the cave opening. No one was there. George walked further out. He kneeled under the cover of a tree. He panned the area. Leaves rustled in the breeze.

Out of the quiet came the sound of horses galloping and men shouting in Spanish.

George ran to Cy. "We have to go! They're coming back!"

He grabbed the saddlebag and helped Cy to his feet. Cy leaned on George until they reached their horses. Cy lifted his left foot to the stirrup. George pushed him up and over into the saddle.

"You always were the strong one, George," Cy said.

"Yeah, and the best shot, too," George reminded him.

"And the best shot, too," Cy replied, managing a weak smile.

The horses trotted through the trees for several miles. When they thought it was safe, they walked them on to Sacramento.

Tired and hungry, they reached Sutter's Embarcadero early the following evening. They lifted their neckerchiefs over their mouths and noses. Cy covered his bloody leg with his duster.

"I'm sure looking forward to a home-cooked meal and a real bed," George said.

"Yeah, Lucy won't care if we spend some of that gold." They both laughed.

George called to a stagecoach driver passing by on Front Street. "Hey, is there a boarding house around here?"

"Wilson's," the driver called back. "Davis and Main Streets."

"How about a stable?"

"Pacific Stables, Second Street. You can't miss it! It's a grand building!"

George lifted his hat. "Much obliged."

"Better keep your hat on, George," Cy warned. "Someone might recognize us. Heck, Lucy might be out here somewhere." George pushed his hat down further. They made their way to Pacific Stables.

When they arrived, a horse groom met them outside. "Are you looking to board your horses?" he asked.

"Yes, sir," George answered.

"For how long?"

"Not sure," Cy replied. "A couple of days, I suppose."

"That works fine," the groom said. He held out his hand. "My name's Morgan." They each shook his hand. "I'll be watching these fine stallions for you. What are your names?"

George was stumped and turned to Cy. Cy said, "My last name's Smith and this is my friend Jones."

Morgan nodded. "All right, Mr. Smith and Mr. Jones, you can pay when you return for your horses."

"Thanks," George said.

They walked on until they located Wilson's Boarding House. It was a simple two-story white house. A sign on the door welcomed guests. A bell above the door jingled as Cy and George entered.

"Hello, there," a woman said from behind the desk. "Welcome. What can I do for you boys?"

"Have you got any rooms for rent?" Cy asked.

"Yes, we do. Are you two going to share?"

"Yes, ma'am," Cy answered.

"Just the room, or do you want supper, breakfast, or both?"

"Both!" George promptly replied.

Luzena chuckled. "My biscuits are famous around here. I think you'll like them."

She passed a ledger, dip pen, and ink for them to register. They each signed with an *X*. "Are you paying with dust?" Luzena asked.

"Depends how much you charge." Cy replied.

"Okay," she said. "I'll forgo weighing the gold dust and charge you each three pinches. One pinch each for the room, one for supper, and another for breakfast in the morning. Sound fair?"

George opened his saddlebag and retrieved the poke bag. There was some dust remaining in the bottom. He reached in, pinched the dust between his thumb and finger, and rubbed six pinches of gold dust, one after the other, into Luzena's poke bag.

"Supper's at five," she said, "in the dining room. And your room is just down the hall, first door on the left." She handed Cy the key. George returned the poke bag to his saddlebag, and they walked to their room. Cy turned the key, and the door opened. They dropped their things on the floor, removed their hats and boots, and flopped on the bed.

George sighed. "Is there anything better than a real bed, Cy?"

Cy was distracted. "We've got to exchange those nuggets for gold coins, George, and we better do it soon."

"Mhm, before we see Lucy and she snatches it from us," George replied.

"Yeah, and before the Joaquins come looking for us, too."

"Lucy told us to let her know when we return," George said. "I'll go down to the Union Hotel tonight after dark and leave her a message."

"Okay, just don't let Lucy see you. And look out for those Joaquins, too. Keep your neckerchief up. Remember, there were wanted posters of us everywhere a couple of weeks ago, and the governor is offering a large bounty for our capture."

"Where should we meet her?" George asked.

"The Stinking Tent, tomorrow," Cy said, "late morning, around eleven. She has our watch now, so she shouldn't be late."

"I'll get that watch back for you, Cy. If it's the last thing I ever do, I will get it back!"

"Well, you know how it is with Lucy. Easy come, easy go, brother," Cy said, "but one thing is for sure. We're not giving her all the gold."

George's face lit up. He raised on one arm, facing Cyrus. "None of it?"

Cy rubbed his chin, pretending to think it through. He grinned and said, "Well, I suppose it won't hurt to give her one nugget." They burst into laughter.

6.

GEE, THANKS, MA!

The Stinking Tent Saloon was quiet the following morning. There was no one at the bar playing dice with the bartender. No one sat at the round tables playing Faro, poker, brag, or three-card Monte. The piano was silent. The lone saloon girl sat on a barstool at the end of the bar and chatted with the bartender, who looked bored with the conversation. She twirled her hair around her finger and yawned now and then.

The men who frequented the saloon would have been there had it not been for the weather. Heavy rain in the northern valley and snow in the foothills of the Sierra made it difficult for prospectors to get to the gold fields. With the confluence of the American and Sacramento rivers just three miles away and no levy to hold it back, the rushing water overflowed onto the streets of the embarcadero. The men were pitching in to repair the damage.

The flood destroyed much property, and many tents blew over and washed away. The businesses housed inside the buildings and tents closed for repairs or replacement. It was a hardship for the business owners. And prospectors could not get the supplies they needed. The Stinking Tent Saloon, however, escaped that level of damage. It stood higher on Front Street, and the owner appropriately anchored it. There were still many puddles inside and outside the tent, and avoiding the puddles was only possible for those in good form. The damp canvas always smelled musty, often causing people to squinch their noses when they entered. It smelled even mustier now. The owner aptly named it the Stinking Tent.

Cyrus and George didn't mind the odor. They walked in and waited for Lucy at a table in the back of the saloon. She strolled in and held up three fingers without looking at the bartender. He wasn't bothered; he understood her gesture. Lucy joined her sons. The saloon girl carried three tumblers full of rotgut and set them down. Lucy took a hardy swig and wiped her lips with the back of her hand.

"Well, what do you have for me?"

"What if I said nothing?" Cyrus replied, glaring at her over his tumbler.

Lucy scoffed. "Cy, you wouldn't have left a note for me unless you had something, so let's not play games. You boys know how it works." She held an open hand toward them. "Hand it over."

George reached into the inside pocket of his duster and pulled out the neatly folded leather poke. Lucy snatched it from his hand.

"Nice poke, Georgie. Did you sew it yourself?" She held it below the table and looked inside. Not believing her eyes, she pulled out three marble-sized nuggets. Lucy's lips curled into a frown.

"Is this all?" she asked. She shook her head in disgust. "How am I supposed to get by with this?"

"What do you mean, Ma?" George exclaimed. "Cy almost got killed over that! It's nothing to sneeze at!"

Lucy raised her arm and waved three fingers in the air. The bartender pulled out a bottle and filled three more tumblers.

"Well, I guess something is better than nothing." She shrugged. "At least it will pay for my hotel and this bar bill." The saloon girl set down the glasses on the table. Cy waited until she was gone, then leaned in.

"That Sonoran, Murietta, is *no bueno*!" Cyrus whispered. "The Five Joaquins and their bandidos? Many men with many weapons. We were lucky to get this much. And to think it only cost me a shot-up leg. But that's no big deal, right, Ma?"

Lucy glanced down at his blood-stained trousers. "You must have been sloppy to get shot. Why didn't you plan it better? And all for three lousy nuggets? I could have done better myself!"

"You?" Cyrus exclaimed. He moved closer and looked her dead in the eye. "You don't do a thing but use us to do your dirty work."

Lucy shrugged it off. "I gave birth to you boys. It's time you do for me."

"Why don't you sell Sutter's pocket watch?" George asked. "I bet you can get a lot of money for it."

Lucy's head snapped toward him. "Why don't you stop talking about that and do as I say?"

"But Ma—" George replied.

"She's right, George," Cyrus said, cutting him off. "We could all be hung for having that pocket watch. You've got to keep it quiet. We've *all* got to keep it quiet."

"Don't worry, it's safe with me." Lucy winked, patting the watch in her sash. She stood up and polished off the rest of her drink. "Get on the Monterey Trail," she said. "Keep your ears to the ground. Talk to the prospectors. Find out who's got gold and go after it. And could you bring it back soon? It's not cheap to live here."

"Yeah, we know," Cyrus replied, with more than a hint of bitterness.

"We're going to need some of that gold back, Ma. One nugget for each of us should do for the time being."

Lucy laughed. "I don't think so, Cy. You see, *you* can get more; it's more challenging for me. Go and find the bandidos again. Only this time, don't come back with three little nuggets." Lucy looked down at Cy's trousers. "Or a bloody leg. I'm positive there's more gold. I hear news of those Joaquins daily."

"They may have seen us," Cyrus replied. "We'll go to the Monterey Trail and see if we can drum up business, but we'll stay away from the bandidos. I'm pretty sure they're after us."

Lucy reached down and pinched Cy's cheeks. She forced a fake smile. "That's what I like to hear, sweet boy." She picked up the poke.

George jumped up. "It sure was good to see ya, Ma!"

Lucy's eyes narrowed. "I'll pay for your rotgut, Georgie, and nothin' more." George beamed a broad, mischievous smile, then did something he'd never done before. He lifted her off the floor and gave her a big bear hug.

"Gee, thanks, Ma!" George exclaimed.

Startled by his show of affection, Lucy pulled back. "Put me down, George!" George put her down. Lucy walked briskly toward the flap door. She forgot about the puddles, which were now mud puddles. She stepped into one of the more enormous puddles. Her boot stuck. She pulled and strained her body. Her bare foot escaped, but not the boot. Every reviled word flew from her mouth. She reached over to grab the boot. She fell in, face first. She cursed everyone and everything. The saloon girl and the bartender were stifling their laughs. Cy and George were speechless.

"Will someone get me out of this puddle?" She looked at Cy and George. Her face contorted with rage. They got up and pulled her out. She wiped the mud from her face, straightened her feather cap, and walked to the door. On the way, she managed to step into several more puddles.

Cy and George waited until she was gone before laughing at the spectacle. "I reckon the bar bill's on us now," George said.

"Yeah, but what a small price to pay for the entertainment!" Then Cy added, "We better take the gold to the assayer soon. Lucy thinks she has all the gold. I want to keep it that way."

"Yeah, but first, I have something for you, Cy." George looked pleased with himself. He moved shoulder to shoulder with his brother. He opened his hand. There lay the gold pocket watch with the initials *J.A.S.*

7.

The End of the Road

The Sierra Miwok established a network of trails long before the Spanish, Mexican, and American people came West to what would become the state of California. During the California Gold Rush, the Lower Monterey Trail was the main route from Sutter's Fort to Monterey. It was prone to constant flooding from the confluence of the Cosumnes River, Mokelumne River, and Sacramento River. A new route further east became the preferred trail for prospectors traveling to the Sierra and back. They called it the Upper Monterey Trail. The trail wound from the Sierra to Sutter's Fort in Sacramento. In between the Sierra and the fort was the Elk Grove Hotel and Stage Stop.

The Lower Monterey Trail abounded year-round with waterfowl, shorebirds, and wading birds. When horses or wagons would pass, vast flocks of white-fronted geese would part and make room for the travelers. Herds of antelope, deer, and elk were ever-present, along with prowling cougars, coyotes, and mountain lions. And it wasn't unusual to spot raccoons, squirrels, and skunks.

In the autumn months, the Upper Monterey Trail, ablaze with colorful fall leaves, was the place to view bald eagles soaring overhead. The gray foxes hunted at night and sunbathed on rocks in the daytime when possible. Snowshoe hares were often seen in the snow, foraging among the brush. Mountain beavers built lodges near slow-moving streams. Ravens taunted them.

Both roads bustled with activity. But the Upper Monterey, with forty-niners fresh from the Sierra, was a bandit's paradise. If thieves could ferret out a specific prospector and knew when and where to make their move, they could become instantly rich and avoid the law.

The Skinner brothers were two of the cagiest thieves on the Upper Monterey Trail. People feared them every bit as much as they feared Joaquin Murietta and his bandidos. Lately, both the Skinners and Murietta were on the Upper Monterey Trail. Because of that, many forty-niners lost their gold and their lives.

"Do you know anyone traveling with gold?" Cyrus scowled, aiming his gun at a lone man traveling east on the Upper.

"No, sir," the man answered, holding his hands up.

George circled his horse closer to the man. "You sure about that?" he asked. "Tell us the truth, you live. Lie, and you die."

"All right, all right." The man's voice was shaky. "A man named Bob Thornton; folks call him Big Bob. He found something this morning on the Cosumnes: big nuggets, lots of them. It could be a rumor, though." The man shrugged. "Last I heard, he was leading his mule west. Could be he was going to the Elk Grove Hotel. It's not far from here."

"What's he look like?" Cyrus asked.

"Big fella, red hair."

"You ain't gonna tell nobody you saw us here, are you?" George asked.

"Oh, no, no. I got nobody to tell. I'm traveling alone."

George looked over at Cyrus. Cy nodded. George cocked the hammer and pulled the trigger. The man dropped. They left him dead, lying in a pool of blood on the road. They rode on and didn't look back.

When the brothers reached the Elk Grove Hotel, it was night. In the sky was a red hunter's moon. Some called it a blood moon, low-hanging and bright. It allowed hunters to stalk their prey at night.

Cy and George tied their horses out of sight in the woods nearby. George grabbed his saddlebag. The gold coins they traded for nuggets jingled in the bag. They crept closer. Cy ran to the back of the hotel. George stayed out front. They hurried from window to door to window, checking the first floor for an entry point. All were locked.

Cy thought it was over and whispered to George. "The only way to gain entrance on the lower level is to break a window, which would alert the owners. We can't do that."

"Look!" George whispered back, pointing to a window on the second floor. A man held a candle. He looked out over the grounds. The candlelight was reflecting the copper color of his hair. He stood there for a while, then blew out the candle.

"He left the window open," George chuckled. "It's like he knew we were coming!"

"That's perfect," Cyrus whispered back. "That tree out front might be hard to climb with my injured leg. There may be a ladder in the stable. Come on." He waved his hand for George to follow.

The wooden door of the stable was easy to slide open. Cy and George felt around in the dark. A horse snorted; a mule chomped on grass hay.

"I found a ladder, Cy," George said. "I think it's a tapering ladder."

"How tall is it?"

George compared the top of the ladder to the top of his head. "I reckon it's six feet."

"It's maybe ten feet from the ground to the balcony," Cy calculated. "If we stand on top of the ladder, we should be able to reach the rail and pull ourselves up. Are you ready to do this, brother?"

"I'm ready, Cy."

"Okay, listen. While I carry the ladder out, you should bury the saddlebag under a bush over yonder." Cy pointed to the bushes along the property line. "Be sure to cover it after you bury it. Mark it some way so we can find it, but no one else can. We'll come back for it later."

Cy carried the ladder out and placed it below the balcony, a few feet beyond Bob's window. George buried the saddlebag in the woods, marking it with a small piece of his dark blue neckerchief. He ran back. They readied their weapons.

"You first," George said. "I'll hold the ladder steady."

Cy climbed up, grabbed the railing, and pulled himself onto the balcony. George followed. They paused and listened for any sound coming from Bob's room. Bob began to snore. Cyrus climbed through the window. George followed. Something, perhaps a table, fell to the floor.

Bob awoke with a start. He sat up and grabbed the bowie knife beneath his pillow. He held the handle in his palm; the blade rested against his forearm. His heart beat fast.

"What's going on?" he asked, squinting in the dark. "Who are you? What do you want?"

"We're here for the gold," Cyrus said.

Bob stood up. "What gold?"

"Sit down," George growled, "and tell us where the gold is."

Bob continued to stand.

"We're not playing around," Cyrus threatened. "Give us the gold."

"I have none," Bob said.

Cy lunged at Bob. Bob fell back on the bed. Cy held a knife to Bob's throat.

"Listen well, or you will die." When he spoke, his spit covered Bob's face.

"I don't know what you're talking about, I swear," Bob stammered.

"Well then, let me refresh your poor memory. Early yesterday morning. The Cosumnes River. Lots of big gold nuggets. Is this ringing a bell, Bob?"

"You must have me mistaken for someone else."

"Are you Bob Thornton?" Bob didn't answer.

"Listen, please," Bob implored, "I don't have any gold. I'm on my way to Sacramento to find work so I can return to Boston. Look around the room. You won't find any gold here."

Cy and George rummaged through the odds and ends of furniture and Bob's belongings. Cy pulled the quilt off the bed. Bob's pistol fell to the floor. Knowing this might be his only chance to get out alive, Bob raised his bowie knife and thrust it deep into Cy's chest. Cy fell on the bed. He exhaled once and lay lifeless.

George drew his revolver. He fired at Bob. Bob fell beside Cyrus. Both lay dead.

George was distraught. He knew he had to go, but without Cyrus, he felt lost. He leaned over his brother's lifeless body and put his hand on Cy's emotionless face. Tears welled up in his eyes. *I'm sorry, Cy. I'm so sorry!* He put one leg out the window and turned back to see his brother for the last time.

"Stop right there!" James Hall shouted from below. George looked over the balcony. A young man was standing beside an older man. Both men pointed their rifles at him. The ladder laid on the ground.

What would you do, Cy?

George rushed to the far end of the balcony. He jumped to the hard ground below. He dropped his gun. He tried standing, but his right leg couldn't bear his weight. He attempted to crawl away, but the searing pain was too much to bear. He closed his eyes and waited for the inevitable.

Instead, the man kicked George's gun away and spoke to him. "What's your name?" James Hall asked, still pointing the rifle at him. George didn't answer.

"That's all right," James said. "I suspect the sheriff will know you. Tie him up in the dining room, John. I'll send a letter to Sheriff McKinney in the morning when the stagecoach arrives."

Sheriff McKinney arrived at the Elk Grove Hotel three days later. He was a young man, tall with dark hair and a thick mustache. He wore a low-crowned hat and a tin badge on his black vest.

The Halls were relieved and grateful to see him. They greeted him outside with eager handshakes. "Hello, Sheriff! I'm James Hall, and this is my wife, Mrs. Sarah Hall."

"Howdy do," he replied, straight-faced. "Where's the prisoner?"

"We had him tied up in the dining room," Mrs. Hall said, "but when the hotel got busy, we moved him to the lean-to kitchen to keep a close eye on him. He jumped from the balcony that night, trying to make a getaway. He broke his leg. I've been doing the best I could to care for it."

"Follow me, Sheriff," Mr. Hall said. "I'll take you to him.

George sat on a chair in the corner of the lean-to. His hands were behind his back, tied up. He was dirty and sweaty. His pants were bloody. The sheriff recognized him right away.

"Well, if it ain't George Skinner." George tried to speak, but the sheriff stopped him. "I've been hearing a lot about you and your brother on the Monterey Trail." He turned to the Halls. "Mr. and Mrs. Hall, let's start with you. Can you tell me what happened here at the hotel?"

Mr. Hall said, "We heard a gunshot in the middle of the night. My son and I grabbed our guns and ran out to the hotel grounds." Mr. Hall pointed to George. "This fellow here was on the upstairs balcony. When he saw us, he jumped to the ground. His leg was badly injured. He tried to crawl away. That's when we grabbed him and tied him up."

"I see. What about you, ma'am?" Sheriff McKinney asked Mrs. Hall. "Anything you want me to know?"

"We only had one guest that night. His name was Bob Thornton. He was staying upstairs in room 202. When James and John ran outside, I grabbed the key and went to his room. I knocked twice, but Bob didn't answer. So, I unlocked the door. Bob and another man were lying side by side on the bed. There was blood everywhere. I tried to wake them, but neither had any life left."

The sheriff nodded. He looked over at George. "Looks like this life of crime has caught up with Cyrus." George looked down. "And it's about to catch up with you, George. Tell me what you and Cy were doing in room 202 that night."

George sighed. "Cy wanted to rob someone. He asked around and found that a man had discovered gold that morning in the Cosumnes. He thought we should go to the hotel and look for him. I didn't want to, but Cy made me."

"Did you know the man's name?"

"Bob Thornton."

"What happened next?"

"Well, we waited until we thought everyone was asleep. We climbed to the balcony and in through the window."

"Go on," the sheriff said.

"Bob told us he had no gold and said to look around the room. So we did. We pulled the quilt off the bed, and Bob's gun fell to the floor. It turned out he also had a knife hidden in his hand. He stabbed Cy to death! And I made him pay for it! I wanted revenge, so I killed him!"

Sheriff McKinney's face was expressionless. "Let me get this straight. You never found the gold?"

"No! I don't know if Bob buried it or what, but we couldn't find it in the room."

He looked at the Halls. "Did either of you find it?" They both shook their heads no.

The sheriff turned back to George. "I'm having trouble here, George. Bob killed Cy because Cy climbed into Bob's room, attempting to steal. Is that right?"

"Yeah," George replied.

"Then you killed Bob because he killed Cy, who just broke into Bob's room to steal his gold. Is that correct?"

"I reckon."

"And after all that killing, no one ever found the gold?"

George saw where this was heading. He was not about to admit guilt. "Sheriff McKinney, I didn't want to rob Bob Thornton. It was Cy's idea. I begged him not to do it. But you knew Cy. He was headstrong, and he could be mean. He was my older brother, and we only had each other for all those years. I couldn't go against him."

"That may explain the break-in," the sheriff said, "but it doesn't explain why you murdered Bob. The way I see it, he did nothing to *you*."

"He murdered my brother, Sheriff. The Bible says an eye for an eye, and I live by the sayings of the Bible."

The sheriff cast a doubtful eye at George. "When was the last time you read the Bible or attended church?" George looked away.

Sheriff McKinney turned to the Halls. "Would you happen to have a sturdy rope?"

"Yes," Mr. Hall said, "there's one in the stable." He left to find it.

"Let's go, George," the sheriff said.

"I can't walk, Sheriff. My leg's broken. It's painful."

"Get up, George, and come with me. It won't hurt much longer."

George leaned on Sheriff McKinney and used his one good leg to hop outside to the oak tree. He took everything in. He heard the crunch of leaves beneath their feet. He saw his breath in the cool morning air. He looked up to the sky. He followed the sun's rays to the trees below. He gazed at each face surrounding him.

George was scared. Tears filled his eyes. But he knew he would be together with Cy again soon, which gave him courage.

Mr. Hall placed the noose around his neck, and soon it was over. Sheriff McKinney suggested to the Halls that they leave his body there for several days to warn others. After a week, they took the putrid body down.

The Halls buried the Skinners and Bob and Jenny in the grave-yard behind the Elk Grove Hotel. They were the first buried there, far from the last.

8.

Lucy Checks In

The office of the *Sacramento Union* newspaper was humming with activity.

Despite the rain, folks waited to hear the promised big news. A tall, thin man wearing a waistcoat and a stovetop hat appeared at the door, waving a newspaper. "Read all about it!" The crowd gathered in closer. He adjusted his oval-shaped spectacles and spoke loud and clear.

"On October 21, 1851, notorious outlaws Cyrus and George Skinner (also known as the Skinner brothers) were killed at the Elk Grove Hotel and Stage Stop in the new town of Elk Grove, California." A cheer went up from the crowd. "According to the hotel owners, the brothers climbed in through a second-story window under cover of darkness and attempted to steal gold from prospector Bob Thornton of Boston. A skirmish ensued, and Bob Thornton killed Cyrus Skinner. George Skinner killed Bob Thornton in retaliation. George Skinner was found guilty by Sheriff Joseph McKinney and hanged.

"It has been reported that Thornton found considerable gold in the Cosumnes River." The man stopped reading and removed his spectacles. "To learn more about the gold, buy today's edition,

91

available from newsies on corners throughout the embarcadero!" The man returned to the newspaper office.

The crowd clapped, and the conversation grew louder. There were two fewer bandits to fear. But for one onlooker, it was the worst possible news.

Lucy stood frozen. *It can't be*, she thought. *Are they confusing my boys with someone else's boys?*

The man returned to the door and held a wanted poster high for the crowd to see. "These posters of the Skinners hung all over the businesses here. I think it's safe to say we can take those down now." Lucy leaned against the brick wall to steady herself. She slowly raised her eyes to the wanted poster.

"Hey," a man cried, "I've seen them around here!"

"Me, too," another man shouted, "at the Stinking Tent!"

"And the River City Saloon!" a young woman added.

Lucy knew she had to leave before she was recognized, too. Her clothing and demeanor had most certainly been a topic of conversation in the saloons. And more than once, she was seen with Cy and George in the Stinking Tent. She breathed a sigh of relief, thankful she wore her duster over her clothes and left her feathered cap in the hotel room. She lifted her neckerchief over her mouth and nose.

Lucy rushed back to the Union Hotel, packed her saddlebag with her meager belongings, and slung the violin case over her shoulder. She hurried downstairs to the front desk and checked out. Untying Prince's reins, she lifted herself into the saddle. When she clicked her tongue, Prince trotted down Second Street.

"Hey, *you!*" she called to a man standing beside a prairie schooner wagon. "You know where the town of Elk Grove is?"

"Yeah, it's south of here, about fifteen miles. It's near the Monterey Trail." Without a thank you or a nod, she and Prince moved on. Lucy had to see the place where Cyrus and George had died.

My boys are gone. She remembered their young faces smiling up at her—serious Cy, with his blond curls and sparkling blue eyes, and George's big smile and funny words that always made her laugh. As they grew, they had many adventures and close calls together. Wanted posters became their calling cards. Sometimes, Lucy referred to them as the Three Musketeers.

Lucy's thoughts turned to anger. *Sheriff McKinney will pay for this! When I find him, he won't live to see another day!*

Then, her anger turned to fear. *But how will I get by without the boys? I have no money and no one else to help me.*

Resolve replaced her fear and anger. *I can do this. I can care for myself like I did in the old days. I'll find the Suisse pocket watch. George took it from me when he gave me that bear hug in the Stinking Tent. He must have had it when he died. I've got to find it. It must be worth a fortune.* She spurred Prince on faster.

Lucy arrived at the Elk Grove Hotel later that day. She rode to the stable and dismounted. Young William Hall welcomed her and took the reins. Walking briskly across the expansive lawn, she entered the building and didn't bother to close the door behind her. No one was at the desk. Lucy tapped the bell. Sarah bustled in.

"Hi there! Are you in need of a room?" Lucy didn't return Sarah's enthusiasm or make eye contact with her. Instead, she gazed around the room and mentally noted anything of value.

"I reckon I am."

"All right, then. Sign here." Sarah handed her the ledger. She slid a dip pen and ink across the desk. "Will you be paying with money, gold, or gold dust?"

"I have a nugget you can weigh," Lucy answered. She signed her name in the ledger, *Lucy S.* Then, opening her saddlebag, she pulled out the poke bag she had taken from Cy and George in the Stinking Tent. She almost felt bad about that now. Lucy reached inside and pulled out a small gold nugget. She handed it to Sarah. Sarah weighed it and returned a coin. Lucy then dropped it in the poke bag.

"You'll be in room 202, upstairs. Let me know if you need anything."

"I do need something more," Lucy replied. "I heard you had two bandits here, both killed. Is that right?"

Sarah's brows knitted together. "Yes, I'm afraid the stories are true. It was the Skinner brothers. They broke into a guest's room to steal gold, and long story short, every one of them died. Such a tragedy. The sheriff hanged George Skinner out front in the oak tree. We buried them out back."

"Is it safe to stay here?" Lucy asked, feigning fear and ignorance.

"Oh, yes," Sarah replied. "We don't expect anything like that to happen again."

"Good," Lucy replied. "Your hotel is very nice. It's a shame for something like that to happen here." She moved on quickly. "What time is dinner served?"

"Five p.m. in the dining room down the hall. Sarah pulled out the newly acquired pocket watch she found in George's belongings. She opened the hunter's cover. Lucy saw it and knew right away it was her pocket watch.

"Is it alright with you if I pay for my meal when I leave tomorrow?"

"That's fine," Sarah said, laying the watch on the desk. She turned to grab the key on the back wall and handed it to Lucy.

"Thank you, ma'am," Lucy said, smiling and winking at Sarah. Collecting her things, she headed upstairs. She pushed the key in and turned it. The door opened.

The air in the room was stuffy. Lucy dropped her things on the floor. She opened the window for fresh air and looked over the front grounds. She paused when she saw the oak tree. A breeze blew through the leaves.

Lucy looked back at the room. Sitting on the organ bench, she ran her fingers over the silent keys. She opened and closed the empty drawers of the highboy chest. She sat on the edge of the bed, testing it for comfort.

Lucy lit the oil lamp on the secretary desk and sat in the chair. She pulled the pocket watch from her vest pocket and turned it over and over. *JAS,* John Augustus Sutter. The watch was all she had now; she hoped it would be worth a pretty penny.

She thought of her boys buried outside in the graveyard. In the morning, she would visit their graves. Despite what Cy and George may have thought, she loved them in her own way.

Lucy couldn't shake the feeling of melancholy. She picked up her violin case and unlatched the lid. Pulling out the violin and bow, she tuned it and played a song in G minor. It was hauntingly beautiful and deeply sorrowful.

Lucy was eight years old and an only child when her mother died. It was devastating. Her father attempted to lift her spirits by playing her favorite tune, "Take Your Time, Miss Lucy. "

When her father died two years later, Lucy went to live with a distant relative. The only items she could take were a few clothes and the violin her father had left her. In her loneliness, she taught herself to play. To this day, her favorite song was still the same.

9.

Dinner Is Served

Joaquin Murietta laughed when he heard that the Skinners were dead. He was confident they were the ones who killed several of his gang and stole his saddlebag full of gold. His next thought was to get the gold back. Since Cyrus and George died at the Elk Grove Hotel, he would make that his first stop.

Two years earlier, in 1849, Murietta was just a teenager when he left Mexico to fulfill his dream of finding gold. But things didn't go as planned. His attempt at gold prospecting didn't pan out, and he was subject to constant discrimination. Murietta tried to find a job doing construction or working with horses as a stable hand, but no one would hire him. Eventually, his only option to survive was taking from others.

California became a state in 1850, and soon after, they passed the Foreign Miners Act to drive out Mexicans. By then, the five Joaquins had banded together and responded by raiding the Sierra, Central, and Sacramento valleys. Robbing prospectors and holding up stagecoaches was their specialty.

Young William Hall was on stable duty early that evening. He was busy caring for the horses belonging to the guests who had gathered in the hotel lobby. They were waiting for the monthly dance in the ballroom to begin.

Will heard hooves pounding the dirt and turned to watch a group of men approaching the stable. They weren't like any guests he had ever seen. They wore wide-brimmed sombreros and suede chaps. The silver on their saddles and sombreros sparkled through the dust. He greeted them and took the reins. Several other horses were already in stalls munching on hay. Empty stagecoaches were outside the stable. As usual, the Joaquins scoped everything out.

The guests, dressed to the nines, were playful in the hotel lobby. Musicians were tuning their instruments in the ballroom. The Hall children carried platters of food upstairs: ham slices, potato cakes, fart and dart beans, and Swiss apple cherry pie. The waiting guests breathed in the mouth-watering smells.

The hotel's front door opened. The five Joaquins, followed by two more bandidos, strolled into the lobby. The room grew quiet. The guests moved aside, clearing a path to the front desk. Mrs. Hall looked up from behind the desk. "May I help you?"

Murietta spoke in broken English. "Eat, ma'am?" he said, patting his stomach. "We pay."

"Y-yes," Sarah stammered. "The dining room is at the end of the hall." She pointed. "Dinner will be ready soon. You can go on down."

"Gracias," Murietta said, tipping his chin.

The Joaquins left the lobby, and Sarah turned back to the crowd. "The dance is about to begin! You may all go up to the ballroom now!"

The guests turned rowdy again. They joked and laughed as they climbed the stairs. When the lobby was empty, Sarah ran to find James. She had to warn him and the children that they would serve unusual dinner guests.

The tables had been covered with white linen tablecloths and set for dinner.

Napkins, knives, and soup spoons accompanied each dinner plate. Butter pats, water glasses, and coffee cups completed each setting. Bouquets of wildflowers in glass canning jars adorned each table. A delicious smell wafted from the kitchen. It filled the room with the promise of something warm and tasty.

Upstairs, the dance was in full swing. A caller prompted the dancers' movements in line, square, and contra styles. The men wore long-sleeved cowboy shirts with a bolo or tie and the famous waist overalls invented by Levi Strauss. Their boots were rounded or square-toed and made of cowhide.

The ladies wore prairie skirts, dresses, blouses, and dancing slippers. The loud thumping of feet in the ballroom resonated in the dining room below.

It was Murietta's habit to find a seat facing the door, his back to the wall. He called it his *estar atento*, lookout. Only one table in the dining room provided a lookout.

And it was occupied. Murietta sat at the adjacent table, and the other Joaquins joined him.

A woman sat in the lookout position. Murietta watched her. *Why has she chosen that table?* he wondered. *Is she watching for trouble, too?*

He noticed her unusual garb but didn't judge. His sarape and sombrero set him apart as well. He was only interested in the way she watched the door.

James and Sarah appeared in the doorway. "Dinner will be ready soon," James said, wringing his hands. "We'll get it to you as soon as possible."

Lucy patted the pocket watch in her doublet. *Sarah hasn't missed it yet. Not too bright to leave it out in the open,* Lucy thought.

James and Sarah entered the room with piping hot bowls of chicken stew. Their daughter, Anne Adelle, followed with warm, yeasty bread. Young Henry filled their glasses with water and mugs with coffee.

Murietta spoke quietly to the Joaquins, then turned to Lucy. "We are the only ones here. Eat with us, ma'am?"

"No," she replied. Murietta turned back. Lucy thought better of it and said, "Wait, I will join you."

"No, we join you, ma'am," Murietta replied. The Joaquins and the bandidos picked up their drinks and moved to Lucy's table. She helped by moving the chairs closer together. Murietta sat down in the lookout position. Lucy would have been annoyed any other day but was more interested in discovering their identities.

The lobby bell rang. Sarah rushed out to welcome the arriving guests. James was left to deal with the dining room. He made an awkward attempt at small talk. "I heard you playing the fiddle earlier," James said to Lucy. Murietta perked up; he recognized the word *fiddle*. "Have you been playing long, ma'am?"

"Uh-huh," she answered. It was clear she wasn't interested in engaging with James.

"You play well," he added. "Maybe you'd like to play with the fiddlers upstairs? There's nothing like fiddle music!" James pointed up to the noisy ballroom above.

Lucy shook her head. "No."

Murietta studied her face. Lines were prominent between her brows. They were the kind of deep wrinkles that develop when a person frowns. He wondered if sadness, anger, or both had caused those lines on her face. Murietta knew those emotions all too well.

"That's all right," James replied, "I'll just go get your apple pie and ice cream ready."

There was something else about Lucy that Murietta couldn't put his finger on. He was usually quick at recalling faces. But after racking his brain, he still couldn't pinpoint it. Had they met before? Had he seen her somewhere else? Or was he wrong?

Upstairs, music and dancing continued. The caller, with his muffled voice, could be heard below. "Promenade left, promenade right, swing your partner, sashay." The dancers' feet clack-tapped to the rhythm and slid along the floor.

The Halls brought dessert to the table. Murietta was still thinking it over. He watched Lucy while eating his pie.

Then, it came to him. He abruptly stood and pounded his fist on the table. His chair fell back on the floor.

"Your face," Murietta said to Lucy. "Face of Cy Skinner. You fiddle in Stinking Tent? Skinners go Stinking Tent." Lucy didn't reply. Murietta went on. "You here. Skinners die here." He put both his hands on the table and leaned toward her. He looked her in the eye and asked, "You mama?"

Lucy allowed herself a wry smile. "And you're Joaquin Murietta."

He narrowed his eyes. "Where is my gold?"

"I don't have it. Besides, last I heard, the gold wasn't yours, Joaquin."

Murietta brandished his weapon. He aimed at her. "*¿Quién eres*? Who are you? *¿Como te llamas*? What's your name?"

As proud and reckless as ever, she raised her chin and lifted her eyes. "Lucy Skinner."

Sarah rounded the door carrying a porcelain platter. She saw Murietta's gun aimed at Lucy and dropped the platter on the floor. It shattered, and porcelain shards flew everywhere.

Startled, Murietta looked away. Lucy grabbed her gun and pulled back the hammer. When Murietta looked back, he stared down the barrel of her weapon. "You'll be the first to die, Murietta!"

Murietta yelled, "¡*Manten tu fuego*! Hold your fire!" Lucy had no idea what his words meant. She kept her aim at him and backed out of the room. The other Joaquins and the two bandidos stood behind Murietta. Lucy knew that if she fired at Murietta, they would kill her. Her mind raced. There was only one option, and it was a long shot: to flee. Lucy turned and ran.

The Joaquins riddled her with bullets. She stumbled down the hallway. A burning sensation filled her chest. Bright red blood seeped onto her doublet and dripped to the floor.

Lucy saw the stairs ahead. *I will be okay if I can get to room 202.* Her knees buckled, and she was weak. She fell on the bottom stair. Her life was dripping away.

She heaved her body up one stair at a time. She paused after each stair, taking in enough air to continue. When she was halfway up, she looked back. A blood trail covered the stairs below her.

The Joaquins still pointed their guns at her. Murietta held his hand up, fingers outstretched, and spoke to them in Spanish. Lucy heard the word *muerta* and knew its meaning: dead woman. The Joaquins, including Murietta, returned their weapons to their holsters.

"If I am a dead woman," she gasped, "then you will die with me." She glowered at Murietta and fired. She continued to fire until the bullets and all her strength were gone. Two men lay dead on the floor.

The last two Joaquins leaned over their leader, "Murietta! Murietta! ¡*Levántate*! Get up!" They tried to rouse him, but it was no use. He moaned and fell silent. He was dead. The remaining Joaquins ran out to the stable. They gathered all the horses, including those belonging to the guests upstairs. They galloped away.

Lucy raised her head to the carnage below. A vision of Cy and George appeared beside her. George pushed her hair from her face. Cy held her hand. Lucy whispered, "I killed Murietta, boys. I'll hide the watch and come back for it later. I'll gather my things and go."

She reached for the stair above. The corner shifted and lifted slightly. She covered the loose corner with the billowy fabric of her breeches. She pulled the pocket watch from her vest and pushed it under the tread. *It's safe. The watch will take care of me.* The visions faded. "Cy? George?" she said. "Where are you?" Lucy laid her head on her arm and closed her eyes.

Like a dream, she recalled a time many years ago before her world turned cold. She was sitting on the grass under the shade of an oak tree. She laughed, watching her two young boys at play. One had curly blond hair and sparkling blue eyes. The other had a round face and a wide grin. Over and over, they rolled down a grassy knoll and laughed until their sides ached.

A tear fell from Lucy's eye, and she was gone.

10.

WHAT GOES AROUND
COMES AROUND

John Sutter jostled back and forth in the stagecoach, traveling to the Elk Grove Hotel and Stage Stop. The roads were dry after several sunny days. Charley Parkhurst was the whip driving the coach. Six sturdy Percherons pulled it. Sutter always insisted on having Charley as his driver, the most skilled whip in the Sacramento area.

Charley drove the coach up to the front entrance. He signaled to the horses and pulled the reins back. When the coach stopped, he applied the brakes with his foot. Charley climbed down from the driver's box and opened the door for Sutter. He held it until Sutter was safely down the steps. He pulled Sutter's carpetbag from the boot and handed it to him.

"See you tomorrow, Charley! I owe you a yard of ale!"

Charley jumped up to the driver's seat. "Yes, sir," he replied, lifting his hat. He drove the six horses to the stable. James was waiting with a fresh relay of horses for Charley's return to Sacramento.

Sutter strolled along the wood path leading to the hotel and walked up the front steps. He turned back and looked over the grounds. The expansive lawn was lush and green. It smelled freshly mown. Sutter breathed in the leafy smell. He noticed daffodil petals reaching up to the sun in the flower beds; the yellow flowers would soon open. A light breeze rustled the oak leaves of the tree fronting the hotel.

After taking it all in, Sutter opened the entrance door and stepped inside. He removed his hat and admired the photos hanging in the passageway. Reaching the lobby, Sutter tapped the bell on the front desk. He set his carpet bag down and waited. He could hear the *pit-pat* of footsteps.

Sarah hurried out of the new secret passageway. James and his sons had dug it the previous year—an arduous task. The passageway ran from the hotel to the grounds near the stable and included several storage rooms. A cellar door built almost horizontally to the ground served as the entrance or exit near the stable. With this addition, Sarah and James felt protected.

Sarah closed the bookcase door and locked it. Taking what appeared to be a book down from the bookshelf, she opened it and placed the key inside. The book was hollow, designed to be a safe box. She returned the safe box to the bookshelf.

Sarah rushed to the lobby. "Hello there! Welcome."

"Good day, ma'am," Sutter replied.

"I suppose you need a room."

"Yes, I do," he said.

"Please sign the ledger." Sarah opened the ledger and pushed it toward him with a quill pen and inkwell. He signed it. Sarah picked up the ledger and read his name.

"John Sutter? *The* John Sutter?"

"Yes, I guess I am," he chuckled.

"Well, isn't this *something! John Sutter!* The man who rescued the Donner Party! And not to mention the discovery of gold at your sawmill! What brings you to Elk Grove?"

"Well, ma'am, I heard you had an occurrence here with the Skinner brothers."

Sarah's face fell. "Yes, I'm afraid so. Many bad things have happened here of late."

"Do you mind if I ask what things? Besides the Skinners, I mean."

"Well, the Skinners were responsible for killing a man named Bob Thornton. Nice fellow. His fiancée, Jenny, came from Boston looking for Bob, only to learn that he had died." Sarah's voice faltered. "When Jenny arrived here, she was sick and died soon after.

"Then, after the incident with the Skinner brothers, a rather unusual woman checked in. She was something. It turned out she was Lucy Skinner, the boys' mother. Lucy killed Joaquin Murietta and some of his bandidos who had stopped here for dinner. Finally, the bandidos killed her. We buried them all out back."

"That's a shame," Sutter replied. "I suppose that's why it's called the Wild West."

"These are trying times," Sarah agreed. "You and I are lucky to be alive."

"I'm sorry to bring it up again," Sutter said. "I'm looking for something, a prized possession taken from me. It's a gold pocket watch with a hunter's cover."

Sarah gasped. "Yes, I know the watch you're talking about."

"Oh good!" Sutter said, relieved. "May I have it back?"

Sarah looked pensive. "I found it among the Skinner brothers' possessions."

Sutter slapped his hands together. "I knew they were the ones who took it!"

"No one came around to claim it," Sarah continued, "and I didn't have a watch, so I borrowed it. Someone took it off this very desk."

Sutter's shoulders dropped. He closed his eyes and sighed. "It was stolen off my desk, too."

"I'm so sorry, Mr. Sutter," Sarah said, tears welling in her eyes. "Please be our guest for dinner tonight. It's the least we can do."

"Thank you, ma'am. You're very kind. I'm going to head upstairs now. Some rest will do me good."

Feeling his age, Sutter reached down and picked up the carpet bag. He walked without hurrying and ascended the stairs with caution. Reaching room 202, he slipped the key into the keyhole and the door opened. The room was clean and pleasant, and the window was open. Fresh, cool air filled the room. He noticed the organ in the corner and wished he could hear music.

He lifted a chair and put it down next to the window. He sat and looked out. Memories came flooding back. He remembered the day his father handed him the watch and bid him safe travels to America. His father died a few years later. Now, the watch was gone, and Sutter felt he was losing his father again.

Later that night, Sutter was startled awake. He sat bolt upright and peered into the darkness. He heard a fiddle playing a mournful tune. Sutter saw something. His heart began to palpitate. A dark figure hovered above him. He reached for his spectacles on the nightstand. With clear eyesight, he sized up the shadowy figure. It was horrendous.

"Who are you?" Sutter whispered.

"Don't you mean who *were* you?"

"Okay, who were you? And how did you get in *my* room?"

"John, John, John. Are you so entitled that you believe you deserve answers? I'm what remains of Lucy Skinner. I don't need to enter through a door any longer." The ghost faded away. A glowing orb appeared in its place. It hovered. Sutter fixed his eyes upon it. The ghost came back into view beside him.

Everything about it was disturbing to Sutter. Its misshapen head hung awkwardly on its narrow neck. Through sunken black holes, it stared into nothingness. A vile grin crept across its decayed face, showing its black teeth and gums.

"Ah, now you see me," Lucy said.

Sutter grew impatient with it. "Why am I dreaming this? And why can't I wake up?"

"You *are* awake, John. What you see before you is what remains of a woman abused, forgotten, ignored, and invisible. Just like many you have known and discarded."

"What do you mean *discarded?*" Sutter replied, growing angrier. He rubbed his eyes and looked again.

Two more hideous ghosts appeared. They were side by side at the foot of the bed. Sutter pulled his knees up and walked his body back against the bedpost.

"Who are they?" he cried, pulling the quilt up.

"Meet Cy and George, John. My sons."

"I was George Skinner," one ghost said. "I died in the oak tree out front. And I was left to hang there for days."

"I warned you not to get sloppy, George!" Lucy exclaimed. She screamed so loud her joints snapped.

The other ghost said, "I died in this room. George and I were doing Lucy's dirty work."

"Why do they *always* blame the mother?" Lucy replied, shaking her wobbly head at the perceived injustice.

"Look," Sutter said, attempting to appease them, "I'm only here to find something stolen from me. I'll leave in the morning."

"Mhm, like you left your wife and five children to fend for themselves in Switzerland so you could come to America and make your fortune? You have quite a history, don't you? What about the Miwok and Maidu you enslaved? You said they needed to be kept strictly under fear. How many did you have whipped, jailed, or executed? And don't forget the Hawaiian Kanakas that King Kamehameha 'gave' you to create your agricultural utopia. You claimed to pay them. Did you?"

"And all you care about is the watch?" Cy said. "How does it feel to have a prized possession taken from you? Imagine how it feels to have your *life* taken."

Sutter looked back and forth at the ghosts. "Please go," he murmured.

"We'll leave for now," Lucy replied, "but mark my words. You will *never* find what you're looking for, John. The watch is mine now." The ghosts cackled wickedly and vanished. The room was quiet and still.

Sutter didn't sleep well that night or any night after that. He retired to his hock farm in Yuba. And no one ever found the gold pocket watch.

Until . . .

EUREKA!

Present Day

I I.

SHOW AND TELL

The dismissal bell rang. The students stood and began talking to each other and stuffing their belongings into their backpacks.

Ryan raised his voice above the chatter. "Remember, the bell doesn't dismiss you. I do." They sat down and were quiet. "Okay, see you all tomorrow," he said. "Go on, get out of here! What are you waiting for?" The students crowded out the door.

Abby and Houdi stayed until the others were gone and approached Ryan. He sat at his desk with a stack of papers to grade. "Hey! What's up?" he asked.

They exchanged a glance. Houdi placed his backpack on a desk and unzipped it.

He took out the watch and handed it to Ryan.

"Strange things happened at the museum today," Abby said. Ryan thought of Mrs. West. Those were her words, too.

He inspected the watch. "Where did you find this?"

"In the museum," Houdi answered.

Ryan was puzzled. "The museum? Where in the museum?"

Houdi sighed. "Let me explain. When everyone went upstairs, I was the last one in line. I saw lights hovering above one of the stairs. I took a closer look. The lights circled down under it."

"Okay," Ryan said, "go on."

"I pulled at the stair, but it didn't move. Then, suddenly, it did, and I could lift it. I pulled it up and saw the lights below, reflecting something down in the space. I wasn't sure I could reach it, but I tried. I put my hand inside, grabbed it, and pulled it out. When I did, the lights vanished. I put the stair back in place again and wiggled it. It wasn't loose anymore."

"Did you see anything else that was unusual?" Ryan asked.

"No," Houdi replied. He avoided eye contact with Abby. He wasn't ready to discuss the ghost in the ballroom.

Ryan looked down at the watch. He opened and closed the hunter cover. "You said there were lights. Can you describe them more?"

"Yes, they were twinkling white lights. "

"And you didn't see *anything* else?"

Houdi shook his head.

"Okay, you two know that I have to take this pocket watch to the Sacramento History Museum, right?"

Houdi nodded. "It doesn't belong to me. It belongs in a museum."

"Okay," Ryan said, "thank you both so much for bringing it to me. I can't tell you how much I appreciate it."

"You're welcome, Mr. K.," Abby said. Houdi nodded.

On their way home, Abby asked Houdi, "Why didn't you tell him about the ghost you saw in the ballroom?"

"Because," Houdi shrugged, "I want to talk to Amelia first." Abby understood. "I'll talk to her tonight. You can come over and be there when I tell her."

Back in the classroom, Ryan opened and closed the hunter cover. He wasn't sure what to make of it. *The lights,* he wondered. *Did Bob lead Houdi to the watch*? He had seen no sign of Bob or Jenny since the refurbishment began. Why hadn't the watch been discovered during the renovation? He had so many questions swirling through his mind. He thought of Mrs. West again and the things she told him earlier. Was it a coincidence that they happened on the same day?

Ryan traced the initials etched in gold and said them aloud. "J.A.S., J.A.S., J.A.S. Who were you, J.A.S.?" It was on the tip of his tongue. He laid the watch down. He put his elbows on the desk and rested his head on his folded hands. He closed his eyes. Nothing came to him.

He opened his lesson plan book and started filling in the schedule.

Tomorrow's history lesson: California Gold Rush continued. Review John Sutter.

Then, as if it fell from the sky, he got it. John Sutter. John Augustus Sutter. Ryan smiled to himself, sat back in his chair, and folded his hands over his chest.

He chuckled and said, "Welcome back, Bob and Jenny!"

12.

It All Adds Up

"Wait," Amelia said, "*where* were you exactly?"

"Walking upstairs," Houdi replied. "I was the last one to go up."

Houdi, Abby, and Amelia sat in a circle on the floor of Amelia's room among the stuffed animals she collected. Outside, rain poured, and wind blew hard against the window.

Amelia was playing catchup, listening to the story her brother and Abby were telling her. "And you said white twinkling lights hovered above the stairs?"

"Uh-huh, on a stair above me. The other kids had already gone up."

Amelia turned to Abby. "Did *you* see it, Abby?"

"No," Abby said, "but I saw Houdi's face when he returned to the bus. He was super upset. That's when he showed me the watch."

"And we gave it to Mr. Kelly after school," Houdi added.

Amelia paused to think. "Good. You guys did the right thing."

Abby nudged Houdi. "I didn't tell Mr. Kelly everything, though. There's more." A knock on the door interrupted him.

"Come in!" Amelia called. The door opened, and Zoey walked in. She was drenched from head to toe.

Zoey, TJ, and Sophia agreed to meet at Amelia's house to study for a math test the next day. Zoey sat on the floor. She looked at each of them and knew something was up.

"What's going on?" she asked. She reached for a stuffed lion and held it in her lap.

"Well," Amelia replied, rolling the word out, "Houdi and Abby went on a field trip today, and something happened."

"A field trip where?" Zoey asked.

"I'll give you one guess," Amelia replied.

"The museum?"

Amelia nodded. "Tell her, Houdi."

Before he could answer, there was another knock. Sophia let herself in. TJ followed her, both of them soaking wet.

"Hi," Sophia said. "It's raining cats and dogs out there, and, as you can see, we had no umbrella because my brother and his side-kick helped themselves to it!"

Zoey put her hand over her heart and looked wistful. "Aww, Chase and Hunter. How I've missed them!"

"Well," Amelia said, "before we have a moment of silence in their honor, little brother here has something to share with all of us." They turned to Houdi. He looked unsure. "It's okay, tell them."

Houdi spoke of the twinkling lights that led to the gold watch under a stair.

His descriptions brought back memories for the four friends. The details were familiar.

"Could this be a new adventure?" Zoey exclaimed. "Just what we need!"

"Wait, there's more," Houdi said. He turned to his sister. "I haven't even told *you* everything yet, Amelia. I saw something else; I'm not sure what it was. It resembled a woman, but it wasn't one. It was creepy. It spoke to me and called me by name."

Zoey gasped, remembering her experience in room 202 the year before. "Was it a ghost, Houdi?"

"I don't know." He shrugged.

"Can you describe it?"

"It was wearing a black shroud. It had long gray hair. Instead of eyes, it had empty black sockets and a colossal mouth hanging open. Gusts of wind blew from its gigantic mouth. It blew me back against the wall so hard it knocked me down!"

"Did anyone else see it?" TJ asked.

"No, just me. I told Abby about it afterward, on the bus."

"Can you remember anything else?" Amelia asked.

"Yeah, it played the fiddle. I mean the violin. It played fiddle music. At first, I didn't see anything, but I could feel it. I heard the music when everyone left to return to the bus. That's when I went back to see who was playing. It spoke to me." The memory made Houdi shiver.

"We saw and heard many things before," TJ said, "but never heard any violin music."

Abby was confused. "What do you mean, TJ?"

"Last year," TJ said, "we were trying to solve the clues in the poetry book. Ghosts appeared to us, too. We've kept it a secret because we didn't want to scare anyone away from the museum."

"We weren't sure anyone would believe us anyway," Zoey shrugged.

"You guys believe *me*, right?" Houdi asked. "Because I swear, I *did* see it, whatever it was."

"I think it was a ghost, Houdi," Amelia replied, "and we believe you. The ghost you saw doesn't sound like the ghosts we saw. But I do think it was a ghost." Zoey, Sophia, and TJ nodded in agreement.

"Can you tell us about the ghosts you saw?" Abby asked.

Sophia said, "One was the ghost of Bob Thornton. An outlaw named Cy Skinner murdered him in the hotel in the 1800s. The other was the ghost of Jenny, Bob's fiancée. She came here from the East Coast trying to find Bob. When she arrived, she was sick and died at the hotel, too."

"You *saw* Bob and Jenny!" Abby exclaimed. "Mrs. West told us about them. Their stuff is on display at the museum."

"Right," Amelia replied, "Bob and Jenny led us to the gold."

"How?" Houdi asked.

Amelia, Zoey, TJ, and Sophia giggled. "It started with white twinkling lights, of course!" Sophia replied.

"It looks like Bob and Jenny led *you* to the watch, Houdi!" Zoey said.

"The question is why?" Amelia replied. "Why did they want Houdi to find the watch?"

"I think there's more to this than we know," Sophia added.

"When Bob and Jenny appear, there's usually a reason. A good reason," Zoey said.

"Did the ghost speak to you?" Sophia asked.

"More like screamed. It said that it wanted its watch back. I held onto it and ran to the bus. Mr. Kelly has it now."

"Man, I thought Bob and Jenny were finally able to rest in peace," TJ said.

"That reminds me of something," Abby replied. "Mr. Kelly told us there's a graveyard behind the museum."

"Excuse me, are you messing with us?" Zoey asked. "I've never heard anything about a grave out there. I've not seen a grave marker either."

"No," Abby replied, "I'm not messing with you. Mr. K. said the proceeds from the Winter Ball will be useful for renovating the stable and the graveyard out back."

"I wonder why workers didn't find the graveyard during the restoration?" Amelia asked. She thought about it more, and her face lit up. "But, regardless of that, is anyone thinking what I'm thinking?"

"Oh yeah," Zoey replied. "I'm in, girlfriend!"

"Me, too!" Sophia exclaimed.

They looked at TJ. "Sure. Why not?"

Amelia asked Abby and Houdi, "Are you two ready for a big adventure?" They both nodded their heads with excitement. "Can you keep it to yourselves?"

"Yes!" they cried in unison.

"Great! Let's find the graveyard," Amelia said. "The rain is supposed to be gone by the weekend, and the museum is closed on Sundays. We can go then." They bumped fists to seal the deal.

Zoey sighed, "And now, we have a test to study for."

"Yeah," Amelia sighed. "We better understand math if we're looking for things to *add up* in the graveyard." They threw stuffies at her.

13.

ALL IN GOOD TIME

On the corner of the strip mall was a clock repair shop. The red exterior with yellow trim had long since faded. On the roof was a large metal weathervane of considerable size. Sitting atop the weathervane was a metal rooster appearing to crow. Below, a sign read *Chronos Timepieces* and under it, *Antique Watches & Clocks, Bought - Sold- Repaired.*

A large window displayed many different timepieces. Vintage wristwatches and pocket watches were in wooden boxes lined with black velvet. Antique and vintage clocks filled out the display. All the timepieces kept time.

Ryan stood before the glass display window and peered at the watches and clocks. Looking past the display and further into the shop, he saw the horologist busy at his worktable in an adjoining room.

The entrance door was glass with a metal frame and handle for easy opening. The sign on the door said *open*. Ryan entered. The sound of the door buzzer startled him.

"Hello," the horologist said. He removed the jeweler's loupe from his head and, turning off the LED light, laid it on his table. He walked with some difficulty to the counter where Ryan waited.

"Can I help you?"

"I hope so," Ryan replied. "I have a pocket watch I'd like you to look at, and hopefully, you can give me some information about it." Ryan pulled the watch from his coat pocket and unwrapped it from a piece of flannel.

The horologist returned to his workspace and grabbed his jeweler's loupe. He fixed it on his head and turned on the LED light. He grabbed a pair of tweezers and shuffled back to the counter. After examining the watch, he set it down under a light to show Ryan its components.

"The bow is intact. That's where you attach the watch to a chain if the owner prefers. The crown is where you wind and set the watch. That's in good shape, too. The pendant holds the winding stem. It's stiff, but that's because no one has wound it for a long time. I think it will loosen up."

He opened the back of the case. "The case holds the guts, the inner workings." He closed it and turned it over. "The bezel holds a glass cover, which protects the dial. And last, you see the hands, which indicate the time, as you know." He looked at Ryan. "I would have to keep it awhile to know how well it works. Sometimes, these old watches don't keep time too well."

The pocket watch with the hunter cover

"Thank you for showing me," Ryan said. "I'm afraid I can't leave it here because it doesn't belong to me. But do you have any idea what it's worth?"

"It is a beauty," the horologist said. "The hunter's cover is perfect, and the painted scene is in great shape. It's a Longine, eighteen-karat gold, and made in Switzerland. Can you tell me more about it?"

"I believe it's from the early nineteenth century. It has historical significance and belonged to a man who was famous during the California Gold Rush."

"I see," the horologist replied, "I hope you don't mind my saying, but I couldn't help but notice the initials etched on the back: J.A.S. That, coupled with the information you've given me, leads me to believe I know who the owner was. Was it John Sutter?"

"Yes, I believe so," Ryan replied. "It hasn't been authenticated yet, but it's going to the Sacramento Historical Museum where they will see to that. Until then, I'd appreciate it if you would keep this to yourself."

"Oh sure, no problem," the horologist said. "People come in here with secrets all the time. Do you have a few minutes to wait while I look at some pricing books?"

"Yes, I do," Ryan agreed. He took a seat and pulled out his phone. He opened the web browser and typed *Sutter and his pocket watch* in the search bar. An advertisement in the *Sacramento Union* newspaper popped up. It was dated December 1851. The ad explained the theft of Sutter's watch and the reward he was offering.

Ryan sat back and thought it over. If Houdi found the watch at the hotel, how would it have gotten there? It made sense that the Skinner brothers stole it from Sutter's Fort and took it to the hotel. The Halls probably found it in their belongings after they died. But who put it under the tread of a stair? And why?

The horologist found what he was looking for. He made a copy of the information on his old photocopy machine. He handed it to Ryan, who thanked him. Ryan wrapped the flannel around the watch and placed it back in his pocket.

As soon as he got in his car, Ryan called Matt. "Hey, you won't believe this," Ryan said.

"Lay it on me," Matt replied.

"Yesterday, I took my class on a field trip to the museum."

"All right."

"After school let out, two of my students stayed behind to show me a gold pocket watch found at the museum. Houdi—you know that kid, right? Amelia's little brother. Anyway, he was the last in line when the class went upstairs. As he climbed the steps, twinkling lights appeared above one of the stairs, then quickly disappeared below it. He pulled at the tread, but it wouldn't move. He tried again, and it came up!"

"How can that be?" Matt asked. "The construction workers checked the stairs during the refurbishment."

"I have no idea. Houdi said there was something in the space below that reflected the lights. He reached in and grabbed it. He brought it back to school, and he and his friend, Abby, gave it to me when school let out."

"What? I can't believe it! And there were lights? Did he describe them?"

"He did, and Matt, they sounded *very* familiar."

"Are you thinking of Bob and Jenny?"

"Yes, I think they're back!"

"Wow!" Matt couldn't help but chuckle.

Ryan chuckled, too. "And there's more. On the back of the watch are the initials J.A.S. I'll return to that in a minute."

"Oh, come on, at least give me a hint," Matt said, sharing Ryan's enthusiasm.

"All right, it's someone from the past. Anyway, I took the watch to a horologist this morning."

"Slow down. A what?"

"A horologist. A person who specializes in timepieces. He said the watch is valuable, especially if there's a hunter's cover, which there is, and even more valuable if there's a painting on the cover."

"Is there a painting?"

"Yes, a hand-painted rural scene."

"Go back to the initials," Matt said.

"It took me some time to get it, but it finally came to me. Given the watch's time period, 1830, plus or minus, and the place it was made, Switzerland, I believe it belonged to . . . Are you ready for this? I hope you're sitting down."

"I'm ready," Matt replied.

"John Augustus Sutter!"

"*No way!* It must be worth a *fortune!*"

"The horologist said the watch is worth seven grand, and that's not considering that it's historical. He said that being historical could raise the value tenfold."

"That's unbelievable, Ry."

"I know! I called the Sacramento History Museum this morning. Of course, I have to turn it over to them, but they agreed to loan it to Elk Grove's Historical Society for the Winter Ball. Of course, we have to take out an insurance policy. I'll need your help with that."

"Yeah, sure, no problem. People from the historical society will come unglued when they see it."

"Yes!" Ryan said. "It will be so cool to have it on display."

"For sure. I'll get on that insurance policy right away."

"Thanks, man, I appreciate it."

"All right, let's talk soon," Matt said.

Ryan ended the call. He pulled out of the parking lot and headed to the museum.

14.

KEEP YOUR EYE ON THE BALL

"Abby! Houdi!" Ryan called from the door of the classroom. The school had just let out for the day. "Can I talk to you two for a minute?" They turned back. Ryan held a stack of envelopes in his hand. "These are invitations to the Winter Ball at the museum." Abby and Houdi glanced at each other, not sure where he was going with this. "I will send them to Amelia, Zoey, Sophia, and TJ. Chase and Hunter are on the guest list as well." He grinned like a Cheshire cat. "You found an heirloom, the gold watch that once belonged to John Sutter! How would you both like to attend the ball, too?"

"Oh yes!" Abby cried, jumping up and down. Houdi was less enthusiastic.

"I plan on sending parents an email with the details," Ryan said, "but so you know, it's this coming Saturday night. And it's a costume ball, so dress as your favorite California Gold Rush character and be prepared to dance!" Then he added, "Oh, and I will call you forward, Houdi, during the ball to acknowledge your part in finding the watch. Let's keep it a secret till then, okay?"

"But Mr. Kelly," Abby replied, "I didn't find the watch. Houdi did. Can I still come?"

Ryan smiled at her honesty. "You were Houdi's moral support, and you both brought the pocket watch to me."

"Okay, Mr. Kelly," Abby replied. "Thank you!"

"Yes, thank you," Houdi said. He wasn't thrilled with the prospect of returning to the museum. Ryan still didn't know about the ghost he encountered in the ballroom. Houdi told himself that maybe it wouldn't happen again, and Amelia and the others would be there if it did. *I'll stay close to them,* he told himself. *And with so many people around, what could go wrong?*

Walking home, Abby and Houdi met up with Amelia, Sophia, TJ, and Zoey.

"Hey guys," Amelia said, approaching them. "How's Mr. K. today?"

Houdi pushed his glasses up. "He's fine."

"He's better than fine!" Abby exclaimed. "After class, he told us he was sending invitations to the Winter Ball at the museum. You're all invited, and Chase and Hunter are, too."

"Cool," Zoey replied, sounding apathetic. "Chase and Hunter are bound to cramp my style."

"What style?" TJ laughed. Zoey rolled her eyes.

"Yeah, they probably will," Abby agreed, "but Mr. K. said it's a costume party. He said everyone would be dressing like their favorite California Gold Rush character. Oh, and he also said there will be dancing. It sounds like fun!"

"I wish you guys could come, too," Amelia said.

"Then your wish has been granted! Mr. K. said that because Houdi found the watch and we *both* turned it over to him, he's inviting us, too!"

"That's awesome!" Amelia replied, high-fiving Abby and ruffling her brother's hair. She noticed Houdi was less thrilled about being included. "You do want to go, don't you, Houdi?"

"Yeah, I guess," he shrugged.

Amelia looked stunned. "You *guess*? Houdi, if you're worried, maybe you should tell Mr. K. what you saw in the ballroom." Houdi didn't reply. "Of course, you don't *have* to tell him, but you might feel more comfortable if he knows."

The rasp and *clickety-clack* of skateboards promised a change in Houdi's mood.

Chase rolled to a stop, pushed down on the tail, and lifted the front of his board.

Hunter rode up at a slower speed behind him. He stepped off and burped a loud, thunderous belch. "Thank you. Thank you very much," he said, taking a bow.

"Dude, you're disgusting!" TJ laughed. "What's wrong with you?"

"Sorry, but a man's gotta do what a man's gotta do! You feel me, JT?" He pounded his chest like an ape and burped again.

"Jeez, man!" Chase said, shaking his head.

"Dude, it could be worse," Hunter replied, pointing at Chase. "You better count your blessings!"

Zoey grimaced. "What do you eat that causes such foul smells?"

"Doesn't seem to matter what I eat, little lady; it's all the same. Today, it was Pop Rocks and Coke. A deadly combo. Probably not my best decision." He belched again.

"Ugh," Zoey grimaced and moved further away.

"Not to change the subject or anything," Sophia said, "but I'm going to change the subject."

"Thank you!" Zoey exclaimed.

"Aw, you have my back, Sophia. I'm touched!" Hunter made a heart sign with his hands and burped again. It sounded like a braying donkey.

"Yeah, *touched* is one word for it," Sophia replied. "Anyway, we just found out that we're all invited to the Winter Ball at the museum. Even you, dork—I mean, Hunter."

"Thank you! That's *fire*, milady! I'll bring my Coke and Pop Rocks. Gotta keep it real."

"In that case, you should stay home," Zoey said.

"No way! I'll be there with bells on!" He stepped on his skateboard. "Later gators. Time to spread the love around." He blew a kiss to Sophia.

"Ew!" she cried.

15.

MIND YOUR OWN BUSINESS

The friends arrived at the museum late Sunday morning. The sun shone bright, making it a perfect day for exploring and a welcome change from the recent winter storms.

The parking lot was empty, just what they hoped for. Now, they could check out the grounds as they pleased. Circling to the back of the building, they gazed over the damp, verdant grass that grew past the museum grounds to Mayor Matt's property beyond it.

"Somewhere out there is a graveyard," TJ said.

"I don't see any grave markers," Sophia said.

"There are no upright headstones, but maybe flat ones," Amelia replied. "And if there are, they'll be buried underneath all this grass."

"The truth is, we're looking for bodies, Sophia," TJ said.

"Funny. Very funny."

"Should we spread out to cover more ground?" Amelia asked. They divided up and waded into the dewy grass, which was squishing beneath their feet.

Zoey tripped and fell. "I meant to do that!"

Amelia chuckled. She walked over and helped Zoey up. "I hope you tripped on a headstone."

Zoey pointed to the grass. "I tripped over those bricks, if you must know. But don't worry about me, I'll live. And thanks for your concern, *everyone!*"

"As long as it wasn't a body," TJ called to her.

Zoey put her hands on her hips. "Is it too much to ask for a little sympathy? I could have died!"

"Hey, guys," Sophia cut in. "I may have found something!" They rushed over. Sophia stood beside a weathered wooden door. The door was positioned horizontally to the ground and built above an angled concrete base. Weeds and grass covered it. Tarnished hinges, nails, and the handle all showed signs of age.

"I wonder what's under there?" Houdi asked, pulling back the grass and weeds.

A shout came from further away. "What are you dweebs up to?" Chase and Hunter rode up on their bikes.

"None of your beeswax!" Sophia called back.

"Well, it's my beeswax *now!*" Chase replied. He dropped his bike on the ground and set out through the damp grass. Hunter followed.

"Whoa, look at all the old bricks," Chase said. "There must have been a building out here at one time."

"It could have been the old stable," Houdi said.

"True," Abby agreed.

"Hey, what's that?" Chase asked, noticing the door.

Houdi shook his head and shrugged. "We're not sure. It's a door of some sort."

Chase grabbed the handle and attempted to lift the heavy door. "It's stuck. Hunter, help me out."

Hunter reached down and placed his fingers under the lip of the wooden door. Together, they pulled. After several attempts, the creaky door broke free. Everyone circled the opening, tapped their flashlights on, and held them over the dark entrance.

"There're steps!" Amelia exclaimed. "We could go down there!"

"Girl, you have lost your mind!" Zoey replied. "Nuh-uh, I'm not going down there!" She folded her arms.

"No, listen. We could divide up," Amelia suggested. "Three can go down, three can wait here, just in case there's a problem, and two can be lookouts at the hotel."

"I don't know, Amelia," Zoey said. "That may not be a good idea."

"Yeah," Chase added, "who knows what's down there?"

"Come on! Where's your sense of adventure?" Amelia begged. "It's *us,* for Pete's sake! It's not like we've *never* done anything like this before! And don't forget the *big* payoff last time. Who knows what we might find?"

"That's what I'm afraid of," Zoey replied.

"Me too," Chase said quietly.

"But it could be something *great!*" Amelia pressed on. "Come on, guys! Let's check it out." They stared into the dark, silently pondering the pros and cons.

TJ was the first to speak up. "So, are we gonna do this or not?" Amelia grinned.

Chase was still unsure. "Maybe the guys can go down while the girls wait up here?"

"Chase!" Sophia cried. "You *did not* just say that! There's no way I'm staying up here." She turned to the girls. "Who's willing to go down there with me?"

"Sophia, I'm not okay with this!" Chase replied. "And Mom and Dad won't be, either."

"Well, Chase, they won't have to know unless *you* tell them!"

"Okay, okay, don't fight!" Zoey cut in. "I'll stay up here with Hunter and TJ. Abby and Houdi, you're new to this, so you can be lookouts at the museum. Alert us if anyone shows up. Chase, Sophia, and Amelia, you go down first. And be careful."

Hunter placed his hands over his heart. His face became a mixture of emotionally moved and somehow demented. "Zoey wants to spend time with *me*," he said. "That brings tears to my eyes." He pretended to sniff and dab his eyes with an imaginary tissue.

Zoey glared at him. "Knock it off, Hunter!"

"Well, okay then, we don't have to talk. We can spend time together in perfect silence."

Zoey groaned. "Ugh! Not *perfect* silence, *complete* silence, got it?" Hunter pointed at her and winked.

"Cut it out, Hunter!" Chase warned. He turned to his sister. "Sophia, will you, at least, let me go down the steps first?"

"If it makes you feel better, be my guest." She held her hand out toward the opening. "But I'll be close behind." Chase walked down a few steps and then looked up. "I'll let you know when it's safe, okay?"

Sophia nodded.

He continued the rest of the way down. The last step landed his feet in a puddle. He cast his flashlight around the area. Brick and mortar walls rose to an arched ceiling overhead. Vertical vents, covered by sod outside, allowed a little light and air to pass through, but not enough. Beyond was a dark tunnel.

"Chase, are you okay?" Sophia called down.

"Yes! There are air vents down here, but grass and dirt cover them. See if you can find a sturdy branch about six feet long and bring it back. I'll see if I can open these vents to give us more air and light."

Sophia stashed her phone in her sweatshirt pocket and ran to search for a strong branch among the trees and the underbrush. She found a sturdy limb that had snapped off in the wind. The broken end had a point like a spear. She ran back to the opening.

"I found one!" She passed it to him.

Chase grabbed it and used the pointy end to free dirt and grass from the vents. More light shined down, and he felt fresh air. He shook the dirt from his hair and dusted off his clothing.

"I think it's safe enough!" he called up. "You can come down now, but be careful. There's no handrail, and the stairs are damp and slippery. There's a big puddle at the bottom of the steps, so watch out for that."

Sophia and Amelia climbed down slowly. Though they tried, they couldn't avoid the puddle. They tapped their flashlights on and circled the area. They had never seen anything like it before. The dark passageway gave them pause. They were nervous but thrilled at the prospect of a new adventure.

Chase pointed up. "Those are air and light vents. Without air, we wouldn't be able to stay here very long. We have light as long as our batteries are working. We'll see if there are more vents in the passageway. I'll take the branch along, just in case. If there aren't any, we'll have to leave soon."

He nodded toward the dark passageway. "Are you ready to see what lies beyond?"

Sitting on the hotel's front steps, Abby and Houdi looked over the grounds. "I wonder what's down there," Abby said.

"I just hope they're okay," Houdi replied. He was anxiously shaking his leg.

"Amelia will be okay, Houdi," Abby said.

Houdi wasn't sure about that. His intuition told him to find her and the others and get out. Something was wrong, and he feared for their safety. The ghost crossed his mind.

"I'll be back!" he said, running toward the museum.

"Houdi, wait! We're supposed to be lookouts." He ignored her and kept running.

He rushed past the others. "Houdi!" Zoey yelled. "What are you doing?"

He climbed down the steps. He tapped his flashlight on. He steadied himself and proceeded down the passageway.

The flashlight illuminated the walls, ceiling, and closed doors on either side. Houdi wondered what was on the other side of the doors. He saw clumps of green grass scattered on the dirt floor. Houdi spotted the open vents above. He knew they were down here somewhere.

Houdi continued down the passage. He heard a creaking sound. He stopped. He heard it again. It was louder. His breath was shallow. He walked a few steps further and saw a door slightly ajar. As Houdi watched, it opened the rest of the way. His curiosity trumped his fear. He stepped closer. And closer. He could feel the ghost's presence.

He knew he couldn't run. Amelia and the others might be in danger. He tiptoed to the door. Holding his flashlight high, he peered inside.

There it was. It hovered above old steamer trunks, facing him. Hollow black sockets stared in his direction. Its mouth hung open and was cavernous; the ghost from his dream and the ballroom.

"Houdi," it said, its raspy voice just above a whisper, "are you here to return my watch?" It reached its gnarled gray hand toward him. "Come closer, Houdi." He squeezed his eyes shut and took a step back. He waited for it to destroy him. But it didn't. Its hand never touched him.

Houdi opened his eyes. The ghost was gone. Twinkling white lights encircled him and became two benevolent spirits. One was a man with red hair. He wore miners' clothing. He tipped his chin to Houdi. The other was a beautiful young woman in a long blue dress. Her smile was comforting.

Bob lifted Houdi and carried him down the passageway. Amelia and Sophia beamed when they saw Bob, Jenny, and Houdi. Bob set Houdi down.

A grateful smile spread across Houdi's face. "Thank you," he said. Jenny and Bob made eye contact with each of them, including Chase, and vanished.

Chase looked like he had just seen a ghost because he had. "Will someone *please* tell me what's going on?"

"Yeah, okay," Sophia agreed. "It's time you and Hunter knew. Let's get out of this hole, and we'll explain everything."

As they walked down the passageway, Sophia said to Amelia, "Looks like we're a gang of eight now."

Chase enters the secret passageway

16.

CIRCLE BACK

"What happened?" TJ asked Houdi.

"Well," Houdi said, "when Abby and I were at the museum, I began to get that spidey sense again. I was afraid Amelia, Sophia, and Chase weren't safe. So I ran back and went down to find them."

Houdi looked over at Abby. "I'm sorry I left you."

"No worries," she replied.

"Anyway, I was going down the passageway and saw a half-open door. I looked inside and saw the same ghost in the ballroom during our field trip. It spoke to me and asked if I was there to return the watch. I didn't know what to do. I don't even have the watch anymore!"

"Wait, you saw a ghost?" Hunter asked.

"Yes," Houdi replied, "I'm sure it was a woman in its lifetime. A scary woman! It hovered above old trunks, reaching out to me. I closed my eyes, thinking I was a goner, but nothing happened. When I opened my eyes again, I saw that lights were all around me. The lights disappeared, and Bob and Jenny were there. Bob lifted me and carried me down the passageway to Amelia, Chase, and Sophia."

"You'll be okay, kid," Hunter said, patting him on the back. "We all get scared sometimes. And you saw a ghost! Who wouldn't be afraid?"

Zoey narrowed her eyes. "*Who* are you, and *what* have you done with Hunter?"

Hunter shrugged it off. "I have my moments. Maybe not minutes, but moments. Besides, the kid was scared. Gotta give him a break." They were glad Hunter had a softer side, even if it didn't last long.

"So Houdi," he asked, "were there ghoulies and ghosties inside the trunks, too?" The others groaned.

Houdi shrugged. He wasn't in the mood for jokes. "I don't know. It happened so fast. I didn't have time to look in the trunks."

"I'm not sure how smart this is," Sophia said, "but there's no one in the museum right now, and we're all here. Next Saturday is the Winter Ball, and this place will be crawling with people all weekend. We could go back down *now*, find the room, and see what's in those trunks."

Amelia looked at her brother. "Are you okay with that, Houdi?"

Houdi's eyebrows furrowed. "Yeah, I guess."

Hunter beamed. "Let's circle back, dudes! I want to see that ghost."

They descended the steps and tapped their flashlights. "Is everyone ready?" Chase asked.

They responded with various forms of yes: sure, yep, yeah.

"Houdi, stay behind me and look for the door, okay?"

"I will, Chase."

They entered the dark passageway. The only sound was their shoes on the dirt floor. Houdi watched for the door. When he found it, he pointed. "There, Chase! That's it!"

They rushed into the room, which had several trunks scattered around the floor. TJ kneeled and opened a brown trunk with leather strapping. The others followed suit. They all rummaged through the items inside.

"Just old, musty-smelling clothes and shoes in this trunk," Abby said, pinching her nose.

"Dishes in this one," Amelia added. She held up a plate with a floral design.

"Just a bunch of junk here," TJ noted, "and I have no idea what any of it is."

Hunter sighed. "Nothing but rusty old tools in this one."

They looked through other trunks. Nothing stood out. When it was down to the last trunk, Zoey said, "I'll do the honors." She flipped up the latches and lifted the lid. Sitting atop the contents was a violin case.

The feeling in the room changed. The mood turned somber. The temperature dropped. Houdi's heart began to pound; something wasn't right. Zoey lifted the case from the trunk.

"Haven't you heard that curiosity killed the cat?" Zoey flinched and dropped the violin case. The ghost returned, threw back its head, and laughed.

"Run!" Chase cried. They ran down the passageway and heard her loud, sinister laugh echoing back.

Two more ghosts appeared in the passage. They were male in their lifetime. One carried a noose around its neck. The other wore a blood-stained shirt. Neither one had shoes.

Jenny and Bob came into view. They pointed the friends in the opposite direction.

"But the exit is this way," Abby cried, "and we don't know what's down there!"

"Just do what they say!" Amelia shouted. They followed Bob and Jenny.

At the end of the passageway, Jenny drew their attention to a small wooden box high on a ledge. Amelia reached up and grabbed it. She opened it. Inside was a tarnished skeleton key attached to a length of twine. Amelia wasted no time.

"Hurry! Find the keyhole!" she said. They scanned the door but couldn't see it.

"Use your hands and feel for it," Chase suggested.

"It's here!" Houdi replied. He pointed to a hole concealed in the dark wood.

Amelia held her breath. She inserted the key and turned it. The lock clicked. The door creaked open at a slow pace. They watched over their shoulders for the ghosts. When the door was open wide enough, they pushed their way through. It was dim inside. The air was heavy.

Zoey peeked around the door. She saw a bookshelf covering the back side. It was full of books.

"Hey, I know this bookcase!" She walked ahead and saw the lobby. "Guys! We're inside the museum!"

"So, this is the inside door to the passageway," TJ said. "And it leads back to where we first entered. Maybe they intended it to be a *secret* passageway between the hotel and the stable."

"Yeah, and maybe a place to store their money and valuables," Chase added. "Maybe even things left here by hotel guests. Or as a root cellar in the wintertime."

"Hold on!" Hunter warned. "Before we go any further, don't move." They watched him examine the corners of the ceiling before focusing on the windows and doors. After that, he moved from room to room downstairs.

"I'll be back in a minute," he called. "Don't move until I get there!"

"Is he all right?" Abby asked.

"Beats me," TJ answered.

Chase shook his head. "I don't know. Maybe he's channeling Sherlock Holmes. All he needs is a magnifying glass and one of those crazy-looking hats."

Hunter rejoined them. "I think it's okay to be in here. The windows and doors are alarmed, but there are no motion detectors. We can't open windows or outside doors, though. We'll have to leave the same way we came in, through the passageway."

"Wow, Sherlock," Sophia said, "I'm impressed! I never thought about alarms."

"Elementary, my dear. I've learned a few things from my dad. He knows all about exterior and interior alarm systems. His official title is Security System Installer."

Zoey narrowed her eyes. "Are you sure you and your dad aren't cat burglars?"

"Most certainly not," he replied. "We don't even like cats."

Houdi missed that conversation. He was deep in thought. He said, "It would only make sense for there to be a way to enter from inside the hotel, too. I think there must be another key and keyhole on this side."

"That does make sense," Amelia said. "It would also make sense that it would be somewhere behind these books."

They unloaded books from the bookshelf. When it was empty, Abby found the keyhole. "Here it is!"

"Is it possible the same key will work on both sides?" TJ asked.

Amelia attempted to fit the passageway key into the bookcase keyhole. It didn't fit. "There has to be another key for this side." They glanced around the door.

"I don't see a box, a nail, or anything holding it, though," Amelia added.

"This is a long shot," Chase said, "but I read once that, back then, they used hollowed-out books to keep valuable belongings. They called them book safes."

In double quick time, they inspected each book. "Here it is!" Zoey cried. "It *was* in a book safe, Chase!" She held up another skeleton key hanging from a piece of twine. She handed it to Amelia.

"Okay, guys," Amelia said, "I have a plan. I can stay here with the hotel passage key. I'll shut the door and try the key. If it works, the door will open. If not, I'll knock on the door, and you guys can open it from your side." She handed the passage key to Chase.

"I'll stay with you, Amelia," Zoey volunteered.

The others returned to the passageway. The door shut at a long, drawn-out pace. Zoey and Amelia waited for it to close.

"Well, well, well, what have we here?" Startled, the girls turned around.

The two male ghosts from the passageway were now inside the hotel. Their corpselike appearance was even more terrifying. Along with the noose and the blood-covered shirt, their eyes were blood-red. Their faces were slate gray. Their lips curled. The foul smell of their bodies was nauseating.

"Whatcha doin' here gals? Have you come for tea?" The ghosts chortled as they moseyed toward them. They stalked the girls like wolves, sneaking up on their prey. Amelia turned back to the lock, fumbling with the key. Zoey stood frozen against the bookshelf, watching the ghosts move closer.

"We saw you in the storage room, missy," the ghost with the noose said to Zoey.

"You got the watch with you?" the bloodied ghost asked. "It's Ma's watch. She saw you, gals, and she won't forget. It's better to hand it over." It reached its gray hand to Zoey.

Amelia looked back at Zoey and grabbed her arm. She pulled her close. Zoey returned from her trance-like state.

"We don't need a key to pass through doors," the ghost with the noose said. "Ma doesn't either. All ghosts can walk right through doors, walls, you name it." They continued to move closer.

It's now or never, Amelia told herself. She did her best to steady her nerves. *You can do this.* She slid the key into the keyhole. It turned. There was a click. The heavy door began to creak open. It moved at a sloth's pace.

"They're coming closer!" Zoey squealed.

"You got that pocket watch, gals?"

"This door is too slow!" Amelia exclaimed.

"Help us!" Zoey yelled to the others through the narrow opening. She kicked and banged on the door as it inched open.

"Give me your hand, Zoey," Chase yelled. She reached through, and he grabbed her hand. He pulled as she wiggled through the narrow opening.

"Hurry, Amelia!" everyone shouted.

Amelia looked back at the ghosts behind her. One reached out and touched her hair. She shivered and screamed. She twisted her limbs through the opening. Chase helped her through. They all ran down the passageway.

The ghosts passed through the door. "Give us the watch, gals! It belongs to Ma!"

"Here they come!" Abby cried.

The ghosts were fast on their heels. Zoey was last in line. It grabbed her from behind. She screamed and fell. Hunter kicked at the ghosts.

Bob appeared. The ghosts faded away. "Run!" he shouted to them. He and Jenny followed them.

Eerie whispers filled the passageway: *It's Ma's! It's Ma's! It's mine!"*

They reached the steps. Chase shouted, "Abby, go!" He boosted her up. "Houdi, go!" One by one, they hurried up, their shoes barely touching the steps.

When the others were safe, Chase turned to Hunter. "Go, Hunter."

Hunter shook his head. "No, bro. It's your turn."

Chase nodded and climbed up. When he was safely out, he reached his hand down to Hunter. An icy wind came out of nowhere, so strong it knocked Hunter to the floor. "You can do it, Hunter! Keep coming!"

Hunter heard a voice behind him. It was the ghost woman. "You can't escape us, Hunter. As long as you're here, you're fair game. We were here in life, in death, and we'll be here for eternity."

Hunter looked back. The three ghosts, standing together, watched him through hollow eyes. Hunter inched his way up the steps against the wind. Chase lay on the ground above and reached both hands down while TJ and Amelia held Chase's ankles to keep him from falling down the hole. Hunter grabbed hold. Chase pulled him up. TJ slammed the door. They ran.

"This way!" Hunter shouted, taking the lead. He knew they had to leave the property. Hunter led them past the hotel and down the path. He didn't stop until they reached the public park. They sat at a picnic table under a shade shelter. Sunlight spilled from the turquoise sky, and clouds were gliding by, sprinkling rain. They were silent, each struggling to catch their breath.

Zoey was the first to speak. "Are you okay, Hunter? That was a close one."

"Yeah," he replied. "Thanks, everyone." Chase leaned in and gave Hunter a side hug.

"Hey, we made it through!" Zoey said. "That's something to celebrate! I think Hunter, Chase, Amelia, and everyone deserves a *big* group hug." They rose and huddled together. They wrapped their arms around each other.

Sophia raised her fist and shouted, "To the Gang of Eight!" The others did the same. Together, they fist-pumped and cheered.

Houdi would need time to understand what had happened. The Winter Ball was almost here. Would Bob and Jenny protect the guests? He feared for all of them.

The last trunk

17.

GET THE BALL ROLLING

An Immigrant Christmas was the theme of the first Winter Ball at the Elk Grove Museum. Outside, evergreen wreaths adorned with lights and gold ribbon hung from the windows and doors to welcome those who were instrumental in saving the hotel and those who had a hand in creating the new museum.

Inside, festive decorations of winter holidays filled the rooms, each representing immigrants who traveled to California from around the world during the gold rush. The parlor guests could sit by the warm fire and listen to a storyteller read "A Visit from St. Nicholas" by Clement C. Moore. An advent wreath with purple and pink candles marked the weeks of December leading to Christmas. A creche, a miniature model representing the birth of Jesus, sat on the table beside it. Eager guests were excited to participate in the Mexican Posada, a reenactment of Mary and Joseph's search for lodging in Bethlehem. Afterward, the weary travelers were treated to warm Mexican hot chocolate.

A menorah for the Jewish holiday of Hanukkah topped a blue and silver table runner in the dining room; its blue and white candles represented the victory of the Maccabees over their oppressors. Next to the menorah were eight brightly wrapped gifts. Guests could play a game of dreidel or checkers with the chocolate gold coins called gelt. Bite-sized potato pancakes, known as latkes, were displayed next to applesauce and sour cream, and there were also donut holes as a dessert treat.

The Lunar New Year, a significant Chinese holiday, was represented in the saloon. A floral depiction of Nian, the monster who wanted to scare away the new year, was on the back bar for all to see. Red lanterns, bright lights, and firecrackers could drive the beast away. Flashing red lights warmed the room. Red envelopes to be filled with cash and given to children by their elders were available to guests. Poppers replaced fireworks, and small spring rolls were tokens of hospitality.

The Miwok groups, native to the area, celebrated their acorn harvest in September. However, the historical society felt it was essential to include their custom of celebrating the harvest with their annual acorn festival. Native Americans in full regalia greeted guests and spoke of their customs before handing out glittered acorns and samples of *sautauthig*, a baked pudding made with blueberries, cracked corn, and water.

Upstairs, a silent auction to benefit the restoration of the graveyard was waiting for guests to arrive and place their bids. In the ballroom, there was plenty of holiday cheer. A buffet table overflowed with appetizers and desserts, and many different warm and cold drinks were available.

Other small bites for guests to try were the cheese-stuffed mushrooms, pork and chive dumplings, shrimp cheung fun (rice rolls), acorn bread, and shrimp-filled deviled eggs. Desserts included *sufganiyot* (jelly donuts), jiandui (sesame seed balls), Indian fry bread with acorn nut butter, and Boston cream pie. Punch bowls with cranberry ice rings were full to the brim with Christmas cheer. Hot chocolate was being served.

The polished dance floor was in the center of the room, waiting for guests to enjoy. A table below a gold balloon arch stood before the lighted windows. Natural greenery dressed the table. In the center was a surprise display hidden beneath a gold cloth. It would surely be a big reveal for the partygoers when the time was right.

To create an 1850s ambiance, Ryan cast period music from his phone to wireless speakers hidden throughout the room. Guests were ready to be treated to rousing songs of the time, including "Joe Bowers," "Betsy from Pike," "When I Left the States for Gold," and "The Dying Californian." The emcee was a dance instructor ready to teach period dances, including the polka, the two-step, the waltz, and the schottische.

After adding finishing touches upstairs, Ryan flew down the staircase and propped open the front door to welcome guests. He dressed as James Marshall, complete with Levi's, cowboy boots, and a fawn wool hat. He carried a gold pan with flecks of fool's gold. Stepping out on the porch, he inhaled the smell of the newly mown lawn, pleased with how everything had turned out. The parking lot was busy with chatter and cars pulling up to drop off guests and find their places. Ryan greeted them at the door with handshakes and hugs, doing his best to guess who their costumes characterized.

Mayor Matt, aka Sheriff Joseph McKinney for the evening, stepped up and offered his hand. Ryan took hold, and the two moved in for a quick hug. "Glad you're here, Matt—I mean Sheriff Joseph McKinney. It wouldn't be a party without the first sheriff in Sacramento County!"

"Well, partner," Matt replied, tipping his low-crowned hat and patting his tin star, "I wouldn't want to be anywhere else." He scanned the grounds. "This place has sure come a *long* way, Ry!"

"Many thanks to you, my friend."

"Likewise," Matt replied.

Familiar voices shouted, "Mr. Kelly! Mayor Fox!" Ryan and Matt turned to see a few of Ryan's students running toward them.

"Look at you!" Ryan exclaimed. "Let's see if I can guess who you are." He pointed to TJ and Sophia. "I'm guessing you two are Bob and Jenny!"

"Yes!" they both exclaimed. After finding Bob and Jenny's belongings the year before, they knew exactly how to pull it off. Sophia was wearing a long blue dress and white gloves. TJ found a red flannel shirt that he tore on purpose, along with some trousers and old boots.

Amelia wore men's clothing, which stumped Matt. "Hmm, I'm afraid you're going to have to help me," he said, rubbing his chin. He looked to the others.

"We don't know either." Sophia shrugged. "Amelia wanted to wait to see if you or Mayor Fox could figure it out first."

Matt shook his head. "Well, partner, I haven't a clue. My job is to keep the peace around here." They couldn't help but laugh at the mayor's commitment to his character.

"I'm Charley Parkhurst!" Amelia exclaimed. "I was a noted stagecoach driver, rancher, and maybe even the first female to vote in California."

"Wow!" Matt replied. "What a great idea for your costume! And you, Zoey? I see you have a long dress and you're carrying books, but I still don't know."

"I'm Elizabeth Scott! Now, let's see if I can get this right. I was born a free Black woman and educated in Massachusetts. I was married and had a son, but my husband died, so my son and I moved to Sacramento during the gold rush. The school board wouldn't let my son attend public school, so I opened a school in my home for him and other Black children. I soon included Native American and Asian American students as well."

"Wow, I'm learning so much! I guess there *was* more to the California Gold Rush than James Marshall and John Sutter!" Turning to Houdi and Abby, he said, "I'm going out on a limb here, but are you behind that white wig and mustache, Houdi?"

"It's me, alright," Houdi beamed. "But for tonight, you may call me Samuel Clemens or, as I prefer, Mark Twain. I'm a famous author. I wrote *Tom Sawyer* and *The Adventures of Huckleberry Finn*."

"You sure did," Ryan chuckled, holding his hand out to Houdi. "It's nice to make your acquaintance, Mr. Clemens."

"I bet you can't guess who I am, Mr. K.," Abby said. Ryan looked at her costume thoughtfully. "Hmm, you look like a pioneer carrying a bag of flour." He looked up, appearing to search for an answer he couldn't find. "I'm afraid I might need a hint!"

"Okay, I'm a great cook, and I make delicious biscuits. A miner once offered me five bucks for one of my biscuits. I hesitated because I thought that was too much to pay; the miner thought I wanted more money. He went up to ten dollars, and I told him we had a deal."

"Luzena!" Ryan cried, fist-bumping Abby. "Luzena Wilson! Very nice to meet you, too! I hope our food will meet your standards." Abby giggled.

"Hey, guys!" Hunter cried, stepping up on the porch with Chase. "Hi, Mr. K., Mayor Fox." Then, turning to the others, he added, "Good evening, losers."

Ryan interjected, "They are *not* losers; they are very important guests!"

"Okay, whatever," Hunter replied, then pivoted. "How about my boy's costume?" He pointed to Chase. "Can you, very important people, figure out who this handsome devil is?"

"It's Chase," Houdi answered.

"I mean his costume, Houdi." Hunter patted Houdi on the head. "Go back to sleep, kid."

"Give us another hint!" Houdi said with enthusiasm.

Chase pretended to clear his throat. "Well, you can see I'm wearing my Levi's because . . . I'm Levi Strauss, the inventor of Levi jeans."

"Very impressive," Ryan replied, clapping his hands together. "And what about your costume, Hunter?"

"He's a pirate!" Houdi said.

"Hold it together, kid," Hunter replied.

"There weren't pirates here during the gold rush," Zoey scoffed.

"There were pirates back then!" Hunter replied. "How do you know they weren't here?"

Everyone burst into laughter, even their teacher and the mayor.

"I don't want to admit this," Zoey said, shaking her head, "but I'm beginning to almost *like* you, Hunter." She quickly added, "Not in *that* way, but in the *friend* way."

"Aw shucks," Hunter said, bowing, "I like you, too!"

"I said *almost*," Zoey added.

"He does grow on you," Chase said.

"That he does!" Ryan added. "I would like to invite all your characters to visit our classroom soon to tell your gold rush stories."

"Even Hunter?" Zoey asked.

"Why not?" Ryan replied. "Everyone loves a pirate. For now, though, come on in and enjoy yourselves. Let's get the ball rolling!"

18.

A Little Song and Dance

After having fun in the immigrant rooms, the friends climbed the stairs. Houdi pointed out where he had found the watch. They hurried down the hall to the ballroom.

Stepping inside, they paused, taking in the sights, sounds, and smells. To them, it was a winter dream. Colorful trees representing different cultures glowed throughout the room. White twinkling lights outlined windows and doors; for a moment, they wondered if Bob and Jenny were there. Gold helium balloons filled the ceiling. Crystal chandeliers illuminated gold tablecloths and chairbacks were tied with oversized gold bows. The floor sparkled brightly. The ballroom was a sea of guests dressed in authentic California Gold Rush costumes. They talked and laughed among themselves.

The gang spotted the hot chocolate station and made a beeline across the room. A tall man with a real walrus mustache was serving. He dressed as a gunslinger. He poured their warm drinks and swirled the top of their mugs with whipped cream.

"That will be fifty dollars apiece, partners. Unless, of course, you want to fight for it." He held his hand over his holster and glared at them. They were confused until he broke into laughter. All but Houdi laughed along with him.

"Too soon, Houdi?" Hunter asked, chuckling. Houdi nodded.

"Hey," Amelia said, "I've been thinking about the secret passageway. Does anyone have an opinion about telling Mr. Kelly and Mayor Matt?"

"The violin case is still down there," TJ said.

"Yeah, and so are the ghosts!" Zoey added. "When I picked up the violin case, the first ghost went crazy!"

Chase moved in closer and spoke softly. "I didn't want to say anything until I knew more. Hunter and I skipped school the other day and went to the museum. We made sure Mr. K. and the mayor weren't there. The docent was a man. I think his name was Louis. We told him we were writing a report for school and needed information about hotel guests during the gold rush. He was helpful and took out the first ledger filled in by the Halls and signed by the guests. He looked at the dates and found a woman named Lucy Skinner."

"Even the docent was impressed by that because it was information he didn't know," Hunter added.

"But," Chase continued, "he did know about the Skinner brothers. One of the brothers killed Bob Thornton. The other brother was hanged for murdering Bob. When we looked at the date Lucy Skinner checked in, it was just a few days after the brothers died. Same last name, same time. The docent said it had to be their mother."

"We went to the library and looked up articles that appeared in the local newspapers at that time," Hunter said. "We found an article about the death of the Skinner brothers. They looked a lot like those ghosts who were chasing us in the passageway. Cy was the one Bob killed with a knife. That's why his shirt was bloodstained. George was the one who killed Bob. He had that rope around his neck. And remember? 'Ma wants her watch back!' And another prized possession was her fiddle."

"Lucy was their mother," Chase went on, "and she died at the hotel, too. But not before she shot the legendary bandit, Joaquin Murietta, and several bandidos. They were notorious thieves and killers. They shot and killed Lucy."

"So," Amelia said, "we've seen Bob, Jenny, Lucy, Cy, and George in the passageway. But not Murietta or any of the bandidos."

"That's right," Chase replied, "and judging from what Mr. K. and the docents have told us, I think we're the only ones who know about the secret passageway."

More guests spilled into the ballroom. The master of ceremonies, aka the dance instructor for the evening, followed behind. He waved and said howdy to the animated guests.

"Welcome, everyone!" he said into the mic. "My name's Bart, as in Black Bart! I'll be your emcee for this evening of celebrating the immigrants of the 1850s and their winter holiday customs." The crowd applauded.

"And how lucky are we to be celebrating here, in the very first building ever built in Elk Grove? Yes, sir, the Hall family built this place in 1850!" The crowd applauded again; Bart waited for the room to settle down.

"Now, you're all invited to make your way to the appetizers *any time*, so don't be shy. Help yourselves to good food and drink!" The crowd applauded once more. "Whew! We'll have a great time here tonight, so let's get this party started!"

There was more applause amid shrill whistles. Bart laughed. "Oh, and I almost forgot! Later this evening, Ryan Kelly and Mayor Matt have a special reveal for us, so stick around for that! For now, though, Ryan has put together a bluegrass playlist for everyone to enjoy. I'm also a square dance instructor, here to teach you dances that were popular in 1849!" He nodded to Ryan, who tapped a song on his playlist. When the music began, Bart said, "All right, everyone, grab your partner!"

"Oh, California" was playing over the Bluetooth speakers.

Amelia spoke to Zoey over the music. "Wanna dance, my partner in crime?"

Zoey made a clumsy attempt to curtsy and joined her on the dance floor. TJ locked eyes with Sophia and leaned his head toward the dance floor. She smiled and took his hand.

"Come on, let's go!" Abby said to Houdi. She didn't wait for him to respond. She grabbed his arm, pulling him to the dance floor.

Chase and Hunter made their way to the appetizers. "Bruh," Hunter said, bopping his head to the music, "this food is fire!" They filled their plates and watched from the sideline as Bart tried to teach the partygoers the old-time waltz. Hunter swept his pirate dreadlocks back over his shoulders. "So, do you think the big reveal will be the pocket watch?"

"For sure," Chase answered. The music changed to "Cotton-Eyed Joe," and Bart began to teach the art of square dancing. The dancers laughed as they tried to remember the do-si-dos while keeping time with the music.

A girl in a long pink pioneer dress walked up to them. "Hey, Hunter, would you like to dance?" He was at a loss for words. He stared at her and didn't answer.

Chase nudged him with his elbow. "Go on! Dance with her!" She took hold of Hunter's arm, and he led her to the dance floor. They found their place alongside the other dancers. Hunter didn't wait for Bart's dance instructions. He started doing the pogo, hopping up and down, up and down. The girl giggled and began hopping with him. Soon, everyone on the floor ditched the square dance for the pogo.

"It doesn't matter how you dance, just as long as you're dancing!" Bart grinned. When the song was over, the tired but happy dancers lined up for something cold to drink. Hunter waved a cringy goodbye to the girl. He joined Chase again. Sweat was dripping down from under his Jack Sparrow wig.

"Do you know her?" Chase asked.

"Yeah, that's Ebony. She's in one of my classes."

"She's cute. I think she likes you," Chase said.

"Nah, girls don't like me. I mean, they like me, but not like that."

"You should ask her to hang out sometime," Chase replied.

"We're just friends," Hunter said. "Besides, you and I are too busy ghostbusting these days. We need to get an Ectomobile, dude."

When the music stopped, Bart handed the microphone to Ryan. Matt stood beside him. "Good evening, ladies and gentlemen," Ryan said. The guests quieted down. "On behalf of the Elk Grove Historical Society, I'd like to thank each of you for coming out this evening. I understand the silent auction is still going strong, so don't forget to put your bids in. Now, as promised, we have something extraordinary to share with all of you." He scanned the crowd. "Houdi, please come up and join us!"

Houdi walked up to his teacher. He turned to face the crowd. Ryan continued. "A few weeks ago, my class came here for a field trip. It was a great learning experience, but *no one* learned more than Houdi. I'll tell you why. While we were here, Houdi found something that someone squirreled away in the hotel's early days. No one even found it during the renovation!" He placed his hand on Houdi's shoulder. "Houdi could have done anything with his find, but along with his friend Abby, they made the responsible choice to turn it over to the historical society. They brought it to me after school the same day. When I looked it over, I suspected who it had once belonged to. Judging from the initials on the back, I pulled out old ledgers from 1850 and 1851. I was looking to see if the person I suspected as the original owner ever stayed here. And guess what? That person did, indeed, stay here."

Ryan rubbed his hands together in anticipation. "So, without further ado, Mayor, please show us what Houdi found!" The mayor lifted the cloth to reveal the pocket watch hanging from a gold hook beneath a gleaming glass dome. A gold watch fob was under it.

Ryan continued. "This eighteen-carat-gold Longine, Swiss-made pocket watch belonged to a man with the initials J.A.S. And that man was . . ." Ryan held the microphone up to the mayor.

"John Augustus Sutter!" the mayor cried. There were gasps from the crowd.

"That's right! John Sutter stayed at this hotel in 1851! We have the ledger to prove it!" The crowd applauded.

"I wish we could say that the watch belongs to *this* museum, but it doesn't," the mayor added. "It's on loan tonight and will be returned to the Sacramento History Museum tomorrow. But somehow, it made its way here, and that's something! Please come up and have a look. And let's give a round of applause to Houdi and Abby for recovering this unique artifact!"

A familiar tingling filled Houdi's body. His heart raced as he searched faces in the crowd. Sweeping his eyes over the room, he landed on *them*. Amelia noticed and followed his gaze.

Lucy, Cyrus, and George were standing among the crowd. They were in human form. George and Cyrus wore deadpan expressions. They folded their arms. Lucy stood between them. She held her pepperbox pistol against her chest. The ghosts turned and walked out.

"Follow them," Amelia said. Amelia and Houdi wove through the crowd, hoping to trail them. They weren't in the hallway. Abby and Houdi looked over the stair landing. There was no sign of them.

"Maybe the porch!" Amelia cried, running down the stairs. Houdi was close behind. Amelia threw the door open. Again, nothing. They peeked into each room. The ghosts were nowhere to be found.

Amelia put her hands on Houdi's shoulders. "We'll talk to the others as soon as possible. Until then, stay close to me, okay?" Houdi was happy to oblige.

19.

JUST FIDDLIN' AROUND

"Thanks a lot, Ryan," Bart said, shaking Ryan's hand. "Please keep me in mind for the next event."

"I will," Ryan assured him. "Thank you, Bart." Ryan waved goodbye from the porch, secure in feeling that the Winter Ball was a success.

The gang of eight volunteered to be a part of the cleanup crew. They were busy upstairs collecting empty glasses, half-drunk mugs of hot chocolate, and dirty plates. Amelia pulled her friends together when all the guests had left the room. "Guys, the Skinners, all three of them, were here tonight. Houdi and I saw them."

"Yeah," Houdi added, "and they were in human form. They blended in with everyone else in costume." He rubbed the gooseflesh on his arms.

"Where'd you see them?" Chase asked.

"It was when Mr. K. showed the guests the watch," Houdi replied. "Abby and I were facing the crowd. I felt like something was wrong, and I looked around the crowd, and the three of them were watching me."

"When Mr. K. finished, they left the room. We followed them," Amelia said. "We looked everywhere, but they were gone."

"They were after the watch," TJ added.

Downstairs, Ryan and Matt reflected on the event.

"Well done, Ry," Matt said. "The reveal of John Sutter's pocket watch was a hit with the crowd!"

"I couldn't miss," Ryan replied, chuckling. "I'm grateful the history museum allowed us to borrow it for the night. It's worth more than money. Even with the insurance we purchased, recovering the full value of that watch would be impossible."

Matt agreed. "Yeah, it's irreplaceable."

Upstairs, the friends were well into the final cleanup stage, wiping down tables and sweeping the dance floor. The pocket watch glistened beneath the glass display. Amelia stopped sweeping and leaned on her broom.

"You know, Houdi, it's cool that you found the watch," she said, eyeing it from across the room.

"It found me!" Houdi replied.

Before Amelia could respond, music began to play. It was no longer music from the gold rush era. A lively, upbeat song blasted throughout the room. Hunter slid to the middle of the dance floor, moving his feet and clapping his hands to the Chicken Dance. He waved his friends to join him.

They dropped their rags and brooms and raced to the dance floor. They laughed and danced until the song ended, and then they laughed some more.

Ryan and Matt heard the commotion. They headed upstairs to see what was going on. They grinned and clapped along. When the song ended, they applauded. The dancers took a bow and laughed until their sides ached.

"Dude, that was *sick!*" Hunter exclaimed.

"Hunter, will you explain how that song reached the speakers?" Ryan asked.

"It must be those pesky hotel ghosts," Hunter shrugged. "You know how mischievous they are."

"I see," Ryan replied. He looked around the room. "Well, this place isn't going to clean itself, and I doubt those pesky ghosts will do it, so back to work, roosters and hens." They picked up their brooms and cleaning rags, still laughing about the dance. "And I'll remember to take my phone this time," he winked.

When the ballroom was clean, they turned off the lights and walked to the stairway. Houdi stopped short. "I hear fiddle music again."

"Mr. Kelly might have done it," Abby replied. "I'll ask him!" She ran and called over the landing. "Mr. K, did you or Mayor Matt cast fiddle music to the speakers?"

"No," he answered. "I turned off the speakers when I was up there."

"Okay," Abby replied, "just checking."

Houdi ran to the ballroom. Across the dance floor, the ghost played a sad tune on the violin. The others ran in behind him. "The pocket watch is *mine!*" it said, then vanished.

"Oh no!" Zoey whispered. "The pocket watch is gone!" She pointed to the glass-covered dome. They looked over and saw it was empty.

"Are you guys done up there?" Ryan called.

"Almost!" Sophia called back.

"What should we do?" Abby asked. "That *thing* has the watch!"

"We have to get it back!"

"You're right," Sophia said. "Mr. Kelly will lose his mind when he finds out the watch is missing."

"Time to lock up!" Ryan called.

"Coming!" Amelia called back.

Chase drew them in closer. "I have an idea. We can pretend we're on our way home. When we're sure Mr. K. and the mayor are gone, we'll turn back and go down the secret passage to see if we can find the watch and the violin case while we're at it."

They headed for the stairs and overheard the mayor and Ryan talking. "The watch will be safe here until morning," Ryan told the mayor. "I'll set the alarm and return for it first thing."

The mayor spotted them. "Is everyone ready for a good night's sleep?"

"Yes," they answered, yawning and feigning fatigue.

"Are you okay getting home on your own?" Ryan asked. "I can drive you."

"Chase and I will walk them home," Hunter replied. "Gotta look out for the young uns." Ryan looked uncertain.

"We live close by," Sophia said. "Our parents know, and they're okay with it."

"There's safety in numbers, isn't that right, Mr. K.?"

"Why doesn't that make me feel better, Hunter?" he replied. They laughed. Hunter pretended it was a dagger to his heart.

The gang said their goodbyes and crossed the parking lot to the pathway. Hiding in the darkness, they saw the mayor and their teacher drive away. They raced back to the outside door of the secret passageway. Chase and TJ lifted the door, and Hunter climbed down first. The others followed.

"Okay," Chase said, "stay together. When we find the room, look for the violin and the watch. We have to find them." He turned toward the darkness and tapped his flashlight. The others tapped theirs and followed.

When they located the room, TJ entered first. Lights were hovering above an open trunk. Houdi rushed over. The violin case was there. He held it high and exclaimed, "I found the violin case!"

Lucy appeared, hovering near the ceiling.

"Well, I never!" she laughed. "Do you think we'll let you get away with this, Houdi? How naïve you all are." Lucy swooped down and met Houdi eye to eye. "It will never happen! *Never!*"

The Skinner brothers showed up. They attempted to wrestle the case away from Houdi. He held on tight as they thrashed him around. Bob appeared next and, with one swipe of his arm, sent the brothers flying across the room. They hit the wall and crumpled to the floor.

Bob turned back. "Listen, ghosts can go anywhere on the property but they can't leave it. Run as fast as you can, and don't stop until you're off the property!"

Jenny appeared next to Bob. "Look deep inside the violin case."

"Thank you!" they called, heading down the passageway. They hurried up the steps. They ran across the lawn and the parking lot to the path. They didn't look back or stop until they were beyond the hotel grounds. Cy, George, and Lucy stood in room 202's window, watching them run.

"It would be a lot different if we could leave the hotel grounds," Cy said.

"Yeah, they wouldn't stand a chance if we could," George replied.

"They have my violin case, you nincompoops!" Lucy shouted. She swatted the backs of their heads. "They *were* on the property, and you two let 'em go!"

"Yeah, Lucy, you're right," Cy scoffed, "and now they have *your* violin case, not to mention—"

"Oh, put a cork in it, Cy!"

20.

IN THE NICK OF TIME

They ran from the dark path to the park. Stopping beneath the picnic shelter, Chase said, "Houdi, you should have the honor of opening the violin case."

Houdi flipped the latches and lifted the lid. The violin and bow rested on a red felt lining. Beside it was a felt pouch. Houdi opened it. Inside was rosin for the bow. He took out the rosin and felt something more. He reached inside. A smile spread across his face. Houdi pulled out the pocket watch. They were overjoyed and high-fived each other.

"Wait," Houdi said, "the lining is loose." He handed the violin and bow to Amelia and pulled back the felt. Gold coins of every size lined the ribs of the case.

"They don't look real," Abby said. "It looks like play money."

"Bob said the ghosts couldn't leave the property," Amelia reminded them. "So, just in case it *is* real, we could leave the violin case at our house and only return the watch to the museum tomorrow. We could give the violin case to Mr. Kelly on Monday."

"That sounds good," Sophia replied. She looked worried. "I don't know about the rest of you, but it's getting late, and

Chase and I should be home by now. Should we go back early tomorrow morning?"

"Mr. K. said he'd be back first thing," TJ answered. "What if we meet here before the sun comes up?"

"Sophia's right," Chase said. "We should all get home before we arouse suspicion. We'll need to sneak out and get back home before our families wake up."

Hunter looked at his clock app. "It says the sun will rise at 6:56 a.m. If we meet here at six, we can get in and out before anyone at home notices anything."

"And before Mr. K. returns to the hotel in the morning," TJ replied.

Chase and Hunter ensured that everyone returned home safely. They all knew it was going to be a restless night. And they had to keep their plan quiet.

They met at the picnic shelter before the sun came up. It was cold and dark, and a light December rain drizzled around them. They wore gloves, scarves, and beanies beneath their jacket hoods. They wasted no time entering the damp, shadowy path that led to the museum. Barn owls hooted, and cats yowled, but they were undeterred.

Arriving, they stood shoulder to shoulder, facing the museum. In the dark, it looked bigger and more ominous, and knowing what waited for them in the passageway made it more frightening.

Zoey sighed. "We better get going." They rounded the building and tramped through the wet grass to the outside door of the secret passageway. Hunter pulled it up. They climbed down and huddled together.

"We have to move fast before Mr. Kelly gets here," TJ said. "Look out for cranky ghosts." They all nodded.

"Won't the ghosts just steal the watch again?" Abby asked.

"Yeah, that could happen. There's no lock on the glass dome," Chase replied. "Even if there was a lock, they may still be able to get it."

"We could wait in the hotel until we see Mr. K. pulling up in the parking lot," Amelia said. "Half of us can go into the passage and close the door so he doesn't discover the secret passageway. The others can hide inside the hotel. When they see him driving away with the watch, those inside the hotel can knock, and the ones in the passageway can let them in. Then we can all leave."

"Good idea," Sophia agreed. "That is, if the ghosts will let us leave."

"Bob and Jenny are here, too," Amelia reminded them. "They haven't let us down yet."

"Hey, I have an idea," Hunter said. "If the grumpy ghosts show up, I'll cast the Chicken Dance to the speakers. That might cheer them up."

Chase laughed. "Well, it *is* true that your dancing will, undoubtedly, scare them away."

"Aw, bruh, why you gotta do me like that?"

"Who will be in the passageway?" Zoey asked. She, Abby, Hunter, and Sophia raised their hands.

"That leaves Amelia, Houdi, TJ, and Chase inside," Zoey said. "Does everyone understand the mission?" They answered yes.

"We need to get going," Chase said. They proceeded down the passageway. They walked briskly to the hotel door. They watched, but they didn't see any ghosts. Zoey grabbed the key and pushed it into the lock. The door clicked and slowly creaked open. They each wiggled through. They raced upstairs to the ballroom, using their phones for light.

TJ looked out the window. "We have to hurry. The sun is starting to rise."

"It's already 6:30," Abby said.

Sophia lifted the glass dome. Amelia placed the pocket watch on the hook. She laid the fob below it. Sophia replaced the dome. They turned to leave.

The Skinners appeared and blocked the doorway. "Well, what have we here, boys?"

"Looks like a pocket watch, Ma," George replied, proud of his answer.

"That it does, son. *That it does!*" Lucy replied, punctuating each word. George grinned, showing his black teeth and gums. Cy was scowling.

"I think I'll just take that watch now," Lucy said, holding her hand out.

Houdi stepped forward. He'd had enough. He stood as tall as he could and puffed out his chest.

"My friends and I won't let you!" he said. "So, move on, you . . . lickspittles!" His friends didn't know the word's meaning or if it was a real word.

But the ghosts knew. And they were angry. "How dare you!" Lucy said. "What audacity."

Houdi didn't back down. "You're all mendacious." Lucy pushed Cy and George forward.

"Do something!" she shouted. They moseyed toward Houdi. Lucy stayed at the door. Houdi didn't care and didn't stop. "You're just a bunch of snollygosters!"

Cy and George lurched forward, attempting to grab Houdi. He and the gang ducked and ran around them. They raced to the door. Lucy was waiting for them.

Houdi called upon his quick wit. He reached into his pocket and held his empty palms up in front of her ghoulish face. She looked from one hand to the other. Houdi extended his hand past her face inside the shroud's hood. He moved slowly; he didn't want to alarm her. His hand grazed her head where her ear once was. She winced. He pulled his hand out and held up a silver coin.

"Here, it's for you," Houdi said. "I made it magically appear." Lucy didn't answer. Houdi smiled and nodded at her. "Lucy, this coin is more valuable than someone else's watch." She paused, then reached out and snatched the coin from his hand. The three ghosts faded away.

The gang left the ballroom. They descended the stairs and watched for Ryan. When he drove into the parking lot, they found hiding places.

He entered and turned off the alarm. He walked upstairs and grabbed the glass dome that held the pocket watch. He quickly descended the stairs and set the alarm again. He walked out the door and shut it behind him. Amelia, Houdi, TJ, and Chase watched him drive away.

Amelia opened the door to the secret passageway. They entered and closed it behind them. They made their way to the exit. When they reached the steps, Bob and Jenny were waiting for them.

"Good job, Houdi," Bob said. "You're a quick thinker, and your magic trick served you well."

"Good job, all of you," Jenny added, smiling.

"We knew you had the strength and courage to deal with the Skinners," Bob said. "And in the future, you'll continue to possess those qualities." Houdi reached his arms out to hug Bob. Bob reached his arms out, too. Houdi and Bob may not have felt each

other's arms, but they did feel each other's compassionate spirit.
There was a kind of magic about it.

Epilogue

Three Days Later

There was a loud jingle as Ryan's entrance disturbed the bell on the shop door. He stepped up to the counter and set the violin case down. The numismatist, an authenticator of coins, stepped out from the back and welcomed Ryan in.

"How may I help you?"

"Well, I have some coins I'd like you to look at." Ryan opened the case and set aside the violin and bow to expose the red felt lining. He peeled the fabric back. Gold coins glistened beneath the overhead light.

The shopkeeper removed his glasses from the top of his head and placed them on his nose. He peered inside. "Do you mind if I ask you about the history of this violin case?"

"I don't know a lot," Ryan replied. "Some of my students found it in an old trunk somewhere."

"I see," the man said. "May I take a closer look at the coins?"

"Be my guest."

The shopkeeper pulled one out and inspected both sides. He laid it on the counter and picked up another. Ryan watched as the man divided the fifteen coins into three groups. When he finished, he pulled out a small book with dog-eared pages. Thumbing through, he found what he was looking for.

He pointed to the first group. "These coins are called Quarter Eagles. They were in production from 1840 until 1929 and worth about two dollars and fifty cents then." He leafed through the book and pointed to the second group. "These are Gold Double Eagle Liberty coins from 1850. Back then, they were worth twenty bucks apiece." He turned the page and pointed to the last group. "And these are 1849 Coronation Double Eagles, and they were also worth twenty back then."

The shopkeeper removed his glasses. "I suppose you're interested in knowing what they're worth today." Ryan could feel his heart starting to beat faster. "The more unique and historical a coin is, the more valuable it will be. These coins fit the bill because they're all in great condition and were minted during the California Gold Rush." He picked up a Quarter Eagle coin. "These are worth up to $30,000 each, again, depending upon the coin's condition. I'm not saying you'll be able to get that much for these coins, but you never know. Five times $30,000 is $150,000." Ryan was speechless.

The man picked up another coin. "Now, these Gold Double Eagle Liberty coins are worth, in mint condition, $7,000." He tapped the calculator. "For a potential total of $37,000." He moved to the last group of coins and inspected both sides again. "Last but not least, these 1849 Gold Coronet Head Double Eagles—" He flashed a happy grin. "You might want to sit down for this because they may be worth somewhere between ten and twenty million each! And just so you know, coins like these are on display at the Smithsonian.

"My advice to you, son, is to go directly to the bank and put these in a safety deposit box until you decide what to do with them." He scratched the information on a notepad and handed it to Ryan.

Ryan tucked the paper in his pocket and replaced the coins in the ribs of the violin case. Flipping the latches closed, he said, "Thank you. I appreciate your help."

"Good luck to you, son."

Ryan returned to his car. His mind was swirling. He pushed the key fob to unlock the door and placed the violin case on the passenger's seat. He shut the door, then thought better of it. Opening it again, he buckled the case in. Driving away, he thought of all the improvements the historical society could make to the museum and the grounds.

"Call Matt," Ryan instructed Siri. He waited for the familiar ring.

Matt picked up, "Hey, Ry."

"I hope you're sitting down," Ryan said.

"I am."

"Matt, you won't believe what I'm about to tell you."

It's worth how much?

THE END?

Amy Gorder

Fact and Fiction

The Elk Grove Historical Society

It is a fact that the Elk Grove Historical Society, using old draw-ings and photos of the original hotel and stage stop, began con-structing the Elk Grove House and Stage Stop Museum in 1985. The replica was completed in 2000. It is located in Elk Grove Park and is open to the public.

The Elk Grove House and Stage Stop Museum

Original Elk Grove Hotel

The Hall Family

It is a fact that in 1849, James and Sarah Hall, along with their five children—John, Henry, Anne Adele, and twins Thomas and William—joined a wagon train on the Overland Trail heading for California. They arrived in Placerville, California, in September 1850. The following November, the Halls left Placerville and settled fourteen miles south of Sacramento, and built the Elk Grove Hotel and Stage Stop, the first building in the area. James Hall is credited with naming the town of Elk Grove after finding elk horns in a grove nearby.

James Hall

Sarah Hall

John Augustus Sutter

It is a fact that John Augustus Sutter (J.A.S.) was a Swiss immigrant who established Sutter's Fort in Sacramento. He became famous after gold was discovered by his partner, James Marshall, at Sutter's Mill in Coloma in 1848. During the gold rush, Sutter saw many of his business ventures fail. Eventually, he moved north to live out his days at his hock farm outside Yuba City.

James Marshall

It is a fact that James Marshall was a carpenter and sawmill operator hired by John Sutter. On January 24, 1848, Marshall discovered gold flakes at Sutter's Mill in Coloma, California. Once word of the discovery hit the newspapers, people throughout the world raced to the gold fields, which changed California forever. Neither Sutter nor Marshall profited from the discovery of gold.

The Skinner brothers

Cyrus Skinner

It is a fact that Cyrus and George Skinner were brothers and Old West outlaws. They were members of Richard Barter's (aka Rattlesnake Dick) gang. In 1856, they stole $80,000 in gold bullion from a mule train in Yuba, California. Barter and Skinner were caught stealing mules to transport the gold and were taken into custody. George buried half the money before he was killed for the crime. The other half was turned over to the law. George refused to reveal the location of the $40,000 he buried, and it remains a mystery to this day. Cyrus and Rattlesnake Dick were imprisoned at San Quentin in 1860. Skinner escaped and fled to Montana where vigilantes tracked him down. A mock trial was held, and he was found guilty. He was hanged the same night in 1864. No photos or drawings of George Skinner were available.

Lucy Skinner

I t's a fact that Lucy Aurora Skinner was the mother of Cyrus and George Skinner. Nothing more is known about her life and death, however. The depiction of her as an outlaw is fictional.

Sheriff Joseph McKinney

McKinney, the first elected sheriff in Sacramento County, was killed during a gunfight in 1850 while he and his deputies confronted squatters barricaded in a house in Sacramento. His end of watch was August 15, 1850.

Joaquin Murietta

urietta was a vaquero from Sonora, Mexico. He was peaceful initially, then driven to revenge after a mob of American miners beat him and left him to die. They hanged his brother and murdered his wife. He vowed to kill as many Anglos as possible and set out on a violent career. The state of California offered a $5,000 reward for Murietta, "dead or alive." He reportedly died in 1853, but this has never been verified. Murietta had a reputation among the Mexican people for giving the gold and supplies he stole to the poor and targeting those he felt were taking advantage of them. This earned Murietta the title of the Robin Hood of the West.

California rangers tasked with beheading Murietta preserved his head as proof the deed had been done.

The Five Joaquins

Hispanic Outlaws of the 1850s

The Five Joaquins were an outlaw gang that operated in California between 1850 and 1853. It was led by five men: Joaquin Murietta, Joaquin Ocomorenia, Joaquin Valenzuela, Joaquin Botellier, and Joaquin Carillo. There were other associates, including Three-fingered Jack, who was believed to be the mastermind behind most of the robberies and murders they committed.

The Northern Sierra Miwok

The Northern Sierra Miwok lived for centuries in the area now known as Northern California. They assembled in small villages along the rivers and streams of the Sierra Nevada and relied upon acorns and fish as the mainstay of their diet. Each village had its specific territory to ensure their need for food, clothing, and shelter would be met. John Sutter envisioned an agrarian society and often enslaved or employed members of the Miwok and Maidu tribes to produce and maintain crops and farmland.

The Maidu People

Maidu leaders with Treaty Commissioners —widely regarded as charlatans who indiscriminately stole land.

For thousands of years, the Maidu people lived peacefully in the Northern Valley of California. With the discovery of gold in 1848, their homelands were destroyed or taken away by colonizers. The population dropped from 10,000 to 330 in just three decades through epidemics and bounties.

The Acorn Festival

The Native American Acorn Festival has been celebrated for hundreds of years. Oak trees have always represented a major part of the livelihood of the Miwok and Maidu. The festival is celebrated in the last week of September and is filled with cultural food, dancing, and activities.

Kanakas

Native Hawaiians known as Kanakas dressed in western cloth-ing.Kanakas were indentured servants often forcibly conscripted by colonizers.

Indigenous Hawaiians, who called themselves Kanakas, were brought from Hawaii to Sutter's Fort in 1839. Eight men and two women had been gifted to Sutter from King Kamehameha when Sutter departed the Sandwich Islands for California. Sutter claimed he paid the men ten dollars a month and offered to send them back to the islands after serving him for three years. Women were not offered the same from Sutter and were assigned to washing, cooking, tending the garden, and caring for the children, some of whom belonged to Sutter.

Charley Parkhurst

Charley Parkhurst was in his late thirties when he sailed around Cape Horn to Sacramento. He became a well-known stagecoach driver. A kick from a horse caused him to lose one eye, leading to the nickname One-eyed Charley. He was married and owned a farm in Watsonville, California. It wasn't discovered until after his death that he had been born female.

He may have been the first woman to vote in a presidential election in 1868.

Heinrich Lienhard

Heinrich Lienhard emigrated from Switzerland to America in 1843. In 1846, he joined a wagon train leaving Independence, Missouri, and after six months arrived in New Helvetia, also known as Sutter's Fort. In 1847, he was employed by John Sutter to tend to the fruit and vegetable gardens at Sutter's hock farm in Yuba. After earning Sutter's trust, he was made mayor-domo at the fort. He left California in 1850, traveling the Isthmus of Panama to New York and back home to Switzerland via England and Germany. He returned to America in 1854 and settled in Madison, Wisconsin, where he lived out his years as a well-to-do farmer and respected citizen.

Levi Strauss

Levi Strauss was a German-American immigrant who founded Levi Strauss & Co. in San Francisco in 1853. His business imported clothing, bedding, combs, purses, and handkerchiefs. He manufactured canvas tents and later patented the new popular style of work pants, riveted XX. They are now known as 501 blue jeans.

Elizabeth Scott

Elizabeth Scott and her family left Bedford, Massachusetts, traveled across the Isthmus of Panama, and arrived in rowdy Hangtown now known as Placerville, California. Her husband soon died, leaving her alone with her son, Oliver, in an unsafe location. They moved to Sacramento, where her son was denied enrollment in public school based on the color of his skin. In response, Elizabeth opened a school in her home. Within months, the school had outgrown her house, and she moved it to a new location where she was able to include Asian and Native American students.

Luzena Wilson

Luzena Wilson and her family traveled from Missouri to Sacramento in 1849. She noticed right away that miners were hungry for a taste of home. While cooking dinner for her family, a miner offered her five bucks for a homemade biscuit. Luzena was stunned by the miner's generosity and hesitated to respond. The miner took her hesitation to mean he had offered too little and upped the amount to ten dollars, which she gladly accepted.

Sutter's Fort

Drawing of Sutter's Fort 1850

Sutter's Fort was established in 1839 as an agricultural and trade colony in the Alta California province of Mexico. Its builder, John Sutter, originally named it New Helvetia (New Switzerland). The actual construction of the fort began in 1841. It was the first non-indigenous institution in the Northern Valley of California.

Sutter's Embarcadero

Sutter's Embarcadero 1860

In 1848, Sutter's Embarcadero was known as the City of Sacramento and the epicenter of the California Gold Rush. The city rapidly grew into a trading center for gold miners outfitting themselves for the gold fields. The waterfront location was prime for commercial success but was prone to flooding from the adjacent Sacramento River. It was also the victim of constant fires from the quickly constructed wood and canvas buildings. In 1862, a project was proposed to raise the city above the flood level. Earth was brought in by wagon, and streets were raised. The original street level is still seen throughout the embarcadero, now known as Old Sacramento.

The Kay

K Street rebranded as the Kay

In 1848, Captain William H. Warner surveyed and laid out the city of Sacramento

in a designed grid with letters and numbers. This area is now downtown and midtown.   The north-south streets are numbered 2nd through 30th Street. What would have been 1st Street is now Front Street. The east-west streets are lettered B-X, except for Y Street which is now known as Broadway.

Residents called K Street the Kay during the gold rush. The Kay was the connection between Sutter's Fort and Sutter's Embarcadero. Before the founding of Sacramento, it was a narrow trail.

The Stinking Tent Saloon

Gold Rush re-enactment of the Stinking Tent Saloon

The Stinking Tent Saloon was a popular location at Sutter's Embarcadero. It earned its name for the musty smell it acquired after the flooding from the Sacramento River. People, mostly men, gathered for games such as faro and three-card monte. Drinks were available from the bar and saloon girls.

The bartender would ask unfamiliar guests if they preferred their drink in a clean or dirty glass. A dirty glass was a clear message to others in the bar. It symbolized a self-proclaimed, hardened criminal.

Acknowledgments

Special thanks to the patient Emerald Books team: Jessica Hammerman, editor-in-chief, finds every extra space, misspelling, and cliché just in the brink of time; Laura Stanfill, marketing, instructor of brand awareness, engagement, and growth. Finally, thank you to Isaac Peterson, writing coach, content editor, illustrator extraordinaire, cover artist, and layout designer, whose words run through my mind as I try to sleep: "Maybe you could..." "Do you think...?" "Is there another way?" and "I like this."

I am forever grateful for their support, diligence, and professionalism.

www.ingramcontent.com/pod-product-compliance
Lightning Source LLC
Chambersburg PA
CBHW031444200726
48289CB00007BB/2211